Deal Gone Dead

A Lily Sprayberry Realtor Cozy mystery

Carolyn Ridder Aspenson

ISBN 10: 1726489868 ISBN 13: 9781726489867

DEDICATION

For Mary Ann Ridder.
Thank you for encouraging my love for mysteries.

MESSAGE FROM THE AUTHOR

While I do my best to provide accurate information regarding the crimes, legalities and situations in my novels, I do sometimes take certain liberties, or as my father used to say, embellish for the sake of the story. That being said, for the most part, my facts are accurate, except where they're not. Where they're not, it is not because of misinformation on the part of my experts, it is for the sake of the story and because I like to keep things interesting.

Please keep in touch with me by joining my newsletter at carolynridderaspenson.com

CHAPTER ONE

Myrtle Mae Redbecker said she loved to cook with her cast iron skillet so, I couldn't help but wonder if that was her plan the day someone decided to whack her over the head with it.

I found my elderly client lying on her old, worn linoleum kitchen floor at ten o'clock Monday morning, the exact time of our regularly scheduled weekly coffee appointment.

"Don't be late," Myrtle said early the day before. "Promptness is important to me."

I understood that about the older woman, and I wasn't late, but it was the last time I'd have to rush to a coffee appointment with my crotchety client. My heart ached for Myrtle, but promptness wasn't my best quality, and the eighty-five-year-old woman wasn't the most comfortable client to work with, so it wouldn't be a lie to say a tiny part of me didn't feel a touch of relief about that. When I realized that sense of relief, it was quickly replaced with guilt. My momma would be horrified to know her little girl felt something just south of joy because of someone else's misfortune. Her voice echoed through my head. You were raised better than that, it said. I silently responded, yes, I was. I apologized to my deceased client, hoping she could hear my heart speaking to her.

I breathed through my mouth and stopped myself from squeezing my nostrils shut as I stood outside Myrtle's old farmhouse along with the gathering crowd. The strong smell of ammonia lingered from what I assumed was the neighbor's chicken coop. The old man likely hadn't cleaned it well or recently, and I worried about the poor chickens. The stench was hard on their little lungs, not to mention the hens' egg production.

The front part of the property was already filled with rubberneckers, but that wasn't hard to do since the house rested on a narrow plot of land that butted up next to its neighbors. The rest of it though extended back for what felt like several miles. It never made sense to me, how my little county was designed. Instead of wide open spaces of land, our lots were piled up close together next to our roads extending behind them to either the next country road or the next plot of land. Closer to town, of course, was different, the lots were normal, but the older properties on the outskirts of the county reflected the original landscapes of when settlers first made it to Bramblett County. My mother once told me she thought that whoever drew up the plot lines in Bramblett County must have sipped a little too much moonshine before deciding where one property ended and another began. Practically every other county in the state had square lots but ours. Ours were so unique that one year at the annual county fair we ran a county competition to see who could come up with a county tag line using that theme. They were all horrible, and the judges couldn't pick. As a real estate agent, I was relieved. Long narrow lots weren't the first selling point I lead with when showing a property to a prospective buyer, and I preferred the county not brag about something I saw more as a hindrance than a benefit.

I ignored the whispers and gossip wandering through the expanding crowd and let my eyes wander over the home of my deceased client. I closed them for a moment and let my mind wander back to my childhood when I'd piddle down the old country road and see the home during its better days, before Myrtle and her husband had aged and couldn't take care of it. I wanted to remember the house that way before it was destroyed and replaced with townhomes or condos.

I adored old southern homes. Each of them told a story, their place in history set in the memories of their town, their families, and the people that knew them. The white wrap around porch with the swing and rocking chairs where the family sat and talked or just spent time together instead of ignoring each other for the bright light of the TV or the hypnotic thrill of the Internet. I adored the rows of matching sized windows with black shutters, how they spoke to me of structure and familiarity. I love the weathered white painted wood siding because I grew up in something similar, and just being near Myrtle's reminded me of mine and the memories of days long gone. My heart ached for my client, but it hurt for something long gone, too; my childhood.

I would have stayed lost in the moment but was immediately jolted out of it when the Bramblett County Sheriff, Dylan Roberts sauntered over.

My heart raced and tiny beads of sweat pooled at my hairline. The familiar fresh and clean, manly soap scent hit my nose and overtook the ungodly ammonia smell right away. My nose was happy, but my heart sunk into the pit of my stomach.

Yes, I'd made the 911 call, and yes, I knew that meant that law enforcement would arrive, so to think it wouldn't be the county sheriff was ridiculous but was it wrong for me to hope a deputy showed up in his place?

He saw me and tipped his brown brimmed hat my direction. "Did you touch anything?"

My desire not to see the sheriff had nothing to do with a lack of respect for the office itself. I didn't even disrespect the position. I actually admired law enforcement. I respected their dedication, their commitment, and their desire to uphold the law.

I just had issues with the person currently holding that position.

The sheriff also happened to be my first—and only love. Granted, that was several years ago in high school and part of college, but first loves weren't easily forgotten, especially when they lived in the same small town. I gathered my composure and pressed my lips together for just a second before I spoke. "No, I didn't touch anything. I watch crime shows, you know."

God bless, I did not really say that, did I?

"Okay then. Stay put. I'll have some questions for you in a bit."

I saluted him and instantly regretted it. Calm, cool and collected obviously wasn't working out like I'd hoped. I pushed a fly away blonde curl behind my ear and wished I could crawl under a rock and hide forever. Too bad Myrtle Redbecker didn't have any rocks big enough to hide my five-foot-four-inch body.

My best friend, Belle Pyott bumped her shoulder into mine. "I saw that."

I hung my head in shame. "Did it look as bad as I think?"

She inhaled deeply and then released the breath slowly while nodding. "Absolutely."

I desperately wanted to disappear right there. "Lovely." I pointed to Myrtle's front door. "I guess things could be worse though, right?"

She nodded, then tucked a curl on the other side of my head behind that ear. "You could be poor old cantankerous Myrtle Redbecker. I can't believe she's dead." She clasped her fingers around mine. "And you found her. Are you okay, Lilybit?"

Most everyone in Bramblett County called me Lilybit even though I'd tried for years to drop the nickname and go by my given name, Lily. Some things stuck, and being the youngest and only girl of four children—who, along with my parents, had all moved away—Lilybit was one of those things that stuck. I tried to appreciate that the name wasn't horrible. I knew other people in town who had it worse. I graduated from high school with a kid named after his father, Richard Madders. The family referred to them both by Dick but used big and little instead of junior and senior. Mr. Madders didn't seem to have a problem with the word choice, but his son sure did. It bothered him so much, he hightailed it right out of town two hours after graduation and hasn't been back.

"Hello? You in there?"

I'd been lost in thought, obviously. "Oh, sorry. I'm fine. I think." Truth be told, I'd never discovered a dead body before, and I wasn't quite sure how I felt. "Maybe I'm in shock. I don't know." I pressed my first two fingers to my neck and checked my pulse. "Feels normal." I didn't mention how it nearly beat out of my chest when Dylan showed up.

"Maybe we should get you checked out anyway?" She placed her palms on my cheeks and forehead. "You're so flushed."

I wasn't sure if that was from finding a dead body or seeing my ex-boyfriend.

Belle popped up on her tiptoes and eyed the growing crowd. "Medic? We need an ambulance or something over here," she yelled. "This woman just found a dead body. She could be in shock."

I hushed her. "I'm fine. Really."

Billy Ray Brownlee, one of the county volunteer paramedics, rushed over, his mouth drawn downward in concern. "You all right Miss Sprayberry?"

I grabbed his bicep and squeezed. "I'm one hundred percent okay, Billy Ray. Belle is just overly cautious. You know how she gets. Don't you go and worry your sweet self, you hear me?"

"You sure?" he asked. "I might could get you a cup of sweet tea and a Band-Aid and fix you on up if you'd like."

Billy Ray was nothing short of seventy-five years old and had been the county volunteer paramedic longer than my twenty-six years alive. He had the kindest soul and biggest heart, but he didn't know a thing about medical care. His sure fire medical cure all for everything was a cup of sweet tea and a Band-Aid. It didn't always heal the wound, but his kindness most definitely helped to heal the heart.

"I'm sure, Billy Ray. Now you go and get to saving other people. I'm fine." Billy Ray's good old boy sweetness brought out the small town southern girl in me every time.

"I don't mind staying with you two pretty ladies. An old man like me don't get all that much joy these days, and I might could use some joy."

Belle gave him a hug. "You definitely deserve joy, Billy Ray. You're just the sweetest man alive, and I am sure there are a lot of women who would love to spend time with a wonderful man like you. Now you go and save one of them. Show them how amazing you are."

He blushed. It was adorable. "Yes, ma'am." He smiled at Belle and I and shuffled away.

"It doesn't matter how old they are, men just melt around you," I said.

"They do not."

"Right. And yes, you're all sugar and spice and all that, but we both know it's that." I eyed her curvy figure and pointed to her face. "And that. God gave you the face of an angel with those blue eyes and perfect cheek bones. Making you nice was just so women wouldn't hate you."

Belle was born and raised in the south, but her roots, as my mother said, were dug up from the north and transplanted in the Georgia clay long after our people settled on the land. The Italian in her personality came out every so often, but it was definitely obvious in her appearance. Her long dark hair and olive skin turned heads, and her southern accent just made her all the more appealing to everyone that crossed her path.

She rolled her eyes and then did something angelic by rubbing my arm and hugging me. "So, what happened? Tell me everything." She rubbed her nose. "But first, what on earth is that smell? It stinks to high heaven out here."

My nose must have adjusted to the stink because I'd forgotten about it until Belle mentioned it again. I reminded her of what happened when chicken coops weren't cleaned.

"Those poor chickens." She rubbed her nose again. "And my poor nose. Anyway, back to you and finding Myrtle. Tell me everything."

"I came to have coffee with Myrtle and update her on the property listing like we'd been doing from the start. She'd told me she'd made a decision on one of the three bidders, and we'd planned to discuss that this morning. I knocked on the door, but she didn't answer. The door was unlocked, so I opened it a crack and hollered in, but she still didn't answer, and that's when I saw the glass on the floor down the hall and—"

"Glass?"

"Yeah, from the back door in the kitchen. Whoever did this broke the glass in the back door to get in. I saw pieces of it on the kitchen floor, and that's when I realized something wasn't right, so I went in and checked."

"Wait a minute. You're saying you saw broken glass on the floor and just walked on in? What if the killer was still in there? You could have been killed."

"I know, but I wasn't thinking about that. I was thinking about Myrtle."

"Of course, you were."

"Besides, I listened before I went in and I didn't hear anything, and it didn't feel like anyone was there, so I thought it was safe."

"It didn't feel like anyone was there? What does that even mean? Are you psychic now or something?"

I rolled my eyes. "No. I just mean it felt okay to go in." I shook my head. "I can't explain it. Maybe I wasn't really thinking straight. I don't know. I just know I saw the broken glass, and I needed to check on Myrtle. It was the right thing to do. And I called the sheriff, and given the circumstances, you should be proud of me for that."

She nodded. "Yes, that was probably smart of you, and yes, I'm astonished that you had the guts to do that, actually."

"Gee, thanks."

A car door slammed behind us. "Where's my aunt? What's going on here?" Jesse Pickett's booming voice reverberated across his aunt's front lawn. "Where's Dylan? Someone better tell me what's going on." Jesse pushed out his chest, and, as my father would say, bowed up, but the trembling chin and wide gave away his fear. Yes, he was angry, but the wide eyes were more afraid than anything.

Fear could drive a man to do worse things than anger could any day.

I cut Jesse off at the front porch steps just shy of the front door. "Jesse, I think you should wait for Dylan to come out." Jesse graduated with Belle and me, and Dylan graduated a few years before. We didn't hang in the same social circle as Jesse, but in a small town, everyone knew everyone. "I don't think you want to go in there."

Jesse was at least a foot taller than my whopping five feet and a few short inches, and he carried more than double my weight on his burly body, so I knew I didn't have any real chance of stopping him if he didn't want to be stopped, but I had to make the effort anyway. It didn't matter. He shoved me to the side, knocking over an old rusted shovel in the process. "Out of my way Lilybit. You ain't telling me what to do."

I picked up the shovel and leaned it against the other side of the window out of his way.

Just then Dylan stepped through the front door onto the porch. He grabbed a hold of

Jesse's shoulder. "You might want to calm down there, buddy."

Jesse worked to shrug his shoulder from Dylan's grip, but the effort was futile. His gaze darted from Dylan's face to the front door and then back to Dylan's face again. "Where's my Aunt Myrtle? Someone said she's dead. Is that true? She's all I got left for family. I need to see her."

My heart sank. I'd forgotten that. Jesse lost his mother, father and two younger sisters in a drunk driving accident on Interstate 85 when I was away at college at the University of Georgia. His grandparents, Myrtle's brother Buford and his wife, were long dead, and Myrtle and her husband Wilbur never had kids. Wilbur died years ago, so she was the last of Jesse's living relatives. Whether the two had a relationship or not, it must have been hard for him to know he'd lost his last living relative.

Dylan placed both hands on each of Jesse's broad shoulders. When he spoke, his voice was a calm whisper. "I'm sorry Jesse, but yes, your aunt is gone. The coroner is in there with her now, but I don't think she'd want you to see her this way, buddy." He shifted their stance and directed Jesse off the porch and toward the side of the house. Belle and I tried to follow, but Dylan shot us a look that clearly read back off.

The small crowd must have read it the same, or they were afraid of Dylan because they all stayed away, too. I wasn't afraid of my ex-boyfriend, but I could understand why the reset of Bramblett County would be. He'd bulked up in the seven years he'd been working in Atlanta, and the innocent smile on his face had been replaced by something similar to a distrusting scowl.

I watched as the men talked, trying hard to read their emotions. Dylan showed very few, but Jesse's were all over the place. Hands in the air, feet stomping, head shaking. His stance, sometimes stiff and straight, clearly defending whatever I couldn't hear him say, and other times shoulders slouching in defeat. When Dylan escorted him to a deputy's car, I feared the worse.

"He's sure surprised to see his aunt's dead," Odell Luna, Myrtle's eighty-something-year-old next-door neighbor said to the person standing next to him. I zoned in on their conversation. "Seems to me he ought to be happy as a pig in slop what with him being the one to get the property and all now."

As the real estate agent of record for the property, I knew that wasn't true, but I didn't say anything at that moment. Myrtle showed me her will and given the possibility of her untimely (as she called it) death, the property had been put in a trust to allow for the sale to be completed to one of the three current bidders with the profits being donated to charity. If none of the bids resulted in a sale, the land would stay on the market through the trust until another purchase agreement was made. She had specifically stated the property and any proceeds from the sale would not go to her nephew, though I wasn't privy to the reasons why.

Did Myrtle's planning for her death mean she feared something might happen to her or was it because she was older and just covering her bases? With her dead inside her home, I couldn't help but wonder. Why would someone want to kill her anyway? As my mother would say, no, she wasn't the sweetest cookie on the tray, but she wasn't the sourest apple in the bunch either. Either way, she didn't deserve to die.

I did a full body shake. I really needed to stop quoting my mother. Not only did it make me sound old, it made me feel old. Besides, it made me miss her terribly. Colorado was a long way away, and I had no plans to visit my parents until after the first of the year.

"I know what you're doing," Belle whispered.

"What?" I whispered back.

"Thinking about your mom. Stop it. She's not dead. Myrtle Redbecker is."

She had a point, but sometimes the distance between Colorado and Georgia felt like the distance between earth and heaven. My parents hadn't moved away that long ago, but I their leaving left a hole in my heart. We'd made it through the rough teenage years and finally reached a place where we could enjoy each other, and then they moved hundreds of miles away. Standing outside of Myrtle's home after just finding her dead on her kitchen floor and then having to call 911 only to have my ex-boyfriend come rushing to the scene—that's a whole lot of emotional stuff wrapped up in one event. I'd love nothing more than to sit on my mom's front porch with a glass of sweet tea and a piece of apple pie and tell her about it, but her porch wasn't in Bramblett County anymore, and that was something I'd have to just get used to.

Billy Ray chuckled, and that brought me back to reality, again. "That ought to make you happy, Odell. Then you don't got to worry none about them big developers coming in and building those condos next to your land."

I bit my lower lip.

Belle tapped my shoulder. "Oh, yes, he does."

"Hush. Don't be starting a battle you know I'm going to have to join."

She giggled. "Yes, ma'am."

My best friend wasn't exactly an instigator, but she wouldn't turn down a chance to get my tail up if the opportunity presented itself. She'd done that since elementary school, and I hadn't dropped her yet, so, I couldn't really complain.

Odell smirked. "Them developers have been trying to talk to me, too. I've been thinking about sitting down with Lily over there and seeing what they have to offer."

I pretended like I wasn't listening, but I did my best to shut out the surrounding noise to zone in on the rest of the conversation.

"Lily's the best. Heard she sold her parents property for a pretty penny. Got enough to afford themselves that big RV and a condominium out in Colorado."

I had sold my parents property for a pretty penny, and yes, they were living the life, but that was because of years of hard work, a strictly followed budget, and my father's excellent investment decisions. My real estate experience was merely the icing on the cake, but I wouldn't deny some of that pretty penny being from my efforts if that meant a new client for the real estate business. If Odell Luna did sign on a client though, the first thing he'd have to do would be clean up that smelly chicken coop. I'd even suggest selling or giving the chickens to someone better equipped to take care of them.

Myrtle wanted those big developers to buy her land, and she wanted those condos. She wanted the deal done and signed, and then she planned to move closer to Atlanta into one of the upscale assisted living communities with the money from the sale and the little bit of cash she said she had tucked away in a safe place.

"Ain't nobody getting my money," she'd said. "It belongs to me, and I plan to live fancy with it up in a big high rise in Alpharetta or Roswell like the rich people do."

I prayed Myrtle had the penthouse apartment in a big high rise in the sky. I also prayed she didn't suffer. Like my momma said, Myrtle wasn't the kindest Bramblett County resident, but I liked her just fine, and I certainly didn't want to see anyone die the way she did, no matter whether I liked them or not.

Sonny Waddell, Myrtle's neighbor on the opposite side of Odell Luna and somewhere around the same age, came marching up to the group. "What in God's name is going on here?" He pulled on his red suspender straps which yanked his baggy old blue jeans up higher on his torso, and well above his rounded belly. "Took me nearly ten minutes to get to my driveway from the red light, and that ain't even a quarter mile. Looks like the whole town's heading out here, too." He glanced around the front yard. "What's that old coot up to? She shoot someone or something?"

Belle choked back a laugh.

"You ain't heard?" Billy Ray asked. "Myrtle's dead. Hit on the back of the head with a cast iron skillet."

Belle flinched and whispered in my ear. "Bless her heart. You didn't tell me that."

"I didn't know if Dylan would want that getting out. They rarely do in the TV shows, you know."

"You and your crime TV shows. You need a hobby."

"She's what?" Sonny yelled.

I don't think Mr. Waddell had his hearing aids in. If he even had hearing aids.

Odell spoke louder. "Myrtle's dead. Deader than a doornail, she is."

Sonny jerked his head toward the front of the house. "She can't be dead. I just saw her last night, and she was fit as a fiddle."

For an old woman with a limp, I thought.

"You don't have to be sick to get murdered," Belle said.

I nudged her.

"Well, it's true."

"At least now you don't have to worry about her selling off the property," Odell said. "Looks like it'll go to Jesse after all."

Sonny's face reddened three shades darker than a ripe tomato. I worried he would have a stoke right there, and one no Band-Aid and sweet tea could fix. "Over my dead body. That good for nothing boy ain't getting one square foot of my property." He grunted and upped the volume of his voice. "I told his aunt last night I'd be dead before I let her take my land, and I sure won't let that boy take none of it either."

Belle whispered in my ear. "What's he talking about?"

"I don't know," I whispered back. "But it doesn't sound good."

* * *

The Sheriff's Office analyzed the scene, and the coroner removed Myrtle's body though the back of the house, keeping the onlookers at bay as Dylan pulled rank and sent the crowd home, many of them leaving begrudgingly. He promised to hold a meeting later in the day to keep everyone informed of the situation. When tragedy struck a small town like mine, the rubberneckers sat and watched like their favorite movie was just released on cable. I'm surprised some hadn't brought popcorn and a cooler full of Coke. I stuck around to answer a few more questions, but Belle went back to our office to attend to our other real estate clients. All three of them.

Old Man Goodson's son, Larry Junior—or Junior for short—had been hanging at the back of the crowd quietly watching everything that happened. I suspected he did so because he and Jesse used to be joined at the hip, and he wanted to see how things turned out.

I always wondered how the two got along. Jesse was the big lug of a man even in high school, and Junior was the skinny kid whose bones threatened to break if he tripped over a rock, but their physical differences aside, their friendship seemed to work, until it no longer did.

Junior stuck around to mow Myrtle's property. The go-to guy for most of the old timers in town property needs, Junior had been tending to Myrtle's acreage for the past few years. Since she'd put the house on the market, she'd wanted to stop, but I convinced her it was more important than ever to keep the yard tidy. Most of the acreage behind the main lot wasn't all that important since it was wooded, but keeping the landscaped area maintained would be appealing to interested buyers if for nothing other than aesthetic reasons. If a property wasn't initially visually appealing, typically the buyer couldn't see past that, even if they planned to tear it down and start from scratch.

Junior checked in with Dylan to get the official Sheriff's Office okay to go ahead and drag his John Deere from his truck and do his thing.

"I need to dig out a few of those old River Birch trees for Mrs. Redbecker first. Those ones on the back edge of the landscaped portion of her property are dying, and she wanted them gone. Made a promise," he said. "And I'd like to keep it."

Before Dylan had a chance to answer, I said, "I'll be working with the trust responsible for the property sale, Junior, and I'm sure they'll want you to continue." I grabbed the shovel next to the window and reached out to hand it to him. "Oh, here, this must be yours then."

"Nope, must be Mrs. Redbecker's."

I put the shovel back where I'd found it. "Oh, sorry."

Dylan nodded. "Don't think that will be a problem. Just do me a favor and stay clear of the inside of the property, you got it?"

"Yes, sir."

Dylan sent Junior on his way and closed the front door. "You got a few minutes?"

I shrugged. "Well, considering my appointment is no longer among the living, I think so."

The left side of his mouth twitched. "I'd like to go over what you did when you got here this morning."

"You mean like reviewing the crime scene?"

He laughed that same laugh I'd spent countless nights crying over trying to forget. "You really need to stop watching crime shows."

How many times did I have to hear that? I had a strong suspicion my face glowed as pink as the polish on my toenails. "I'll think about it."

"Did Myrtle mention anything about her nephew and their relationship?"

"Let me guess, you think Jesse killed her, don't you?"

"This is a lot of land. I'm not sure how much an acre goes for nowadays, but I'm guessing it'll sell for a pretty penny."

"He's not named in the will."

"A will can be contested."

"I don't really know the details, but I do know Myrtle was pretty adamant that her nephew not get any profit from the sale. Whatever she didn't use or wasn't specified in the will she said would go to charity."

"That must have upset Jesse."

"I have no idea."

He rubbed his hands together. "So, let's start from the beginning. You come over, and what? Knock on the door?"

I nodded. "Myrtle wanted a regular Monday morning coffee appointment to discuss the update on the sale of her property, even if there wasn't an update." My throat tightened. "I think she was just lonely and wanted the company."

"Probably. Obviously, she and Jesse weren't close, and she didn't have a reputation for being the most pleasant person in town."

"No, she definitely didn't." I exhaled. "But this time we had a reason for the meeting."

"Which was?"

"She's got three bidders vying for the property. All are builders looking to build multi-housing units like condos, and she'd made a decision on which bidder she decided to sell the property to."

"She tell you that?"

"On the phone, yes. Just not which bidder, though I have a pretty good idea." I didn't offer him anything else about the bidders, and he didn't ask. "So, I knocked, but she didn't answer. I checked the door, and it was unlocked, so I cracked it open a bit and yelled in for her, but of course, she didn't answer that either. That's when I noticed the glass pieces on the kitchen floor. I worried she might have fallen or something, so I went in to check. I saw the glass was actually from the backdoor window, and when I got closer, that's when I saw Myrtle lying on the floor. I could tell she wasn't alive anymore, but I checked for a pulse just in case. There wasn't one." I wiped a tear from my eye. I hadn't even realized I'd started to cry. "And then I called 9-1-1."

"You didn't see or hear anyone in the house? Didn't touch anything?"

I shook my head. "Not that I'm aware of, but I wasn't in here for long."

"You've been here before, correct?"

I nodded. "Several times."

He opened the front door for me, but I hesitated before entering.

"You okay?"

I cupped my left elbow with my right hand and nodded. "Yeah, I think so. It's just weird. Someone died in here."

He nodded. "Do you need a minute?"

I shook my head. "I'd rather just get it over with." I took a deep breath and walked inside. It was one thing to watch a fictional crime investigation on TV but entirely different to be a part of a real one.

I glanced around the house and though everything was the same, it was all different, too. The rooms felt different. The air had a thicker feel to it, and when I breathed, I almost had to swallow over letting it just float through my nostrils like it normally did.

"Why does everything feel different?"

"What do you mean?"

"Like the air. It's—" I paused, trying to find a way to explain what I meant. "It's thicker, heavier, and it's got a weird smell to it now."

"Like metal maybe?"

"I…I don't know. I don't really remember it smelling before when I came in and found Myrtle."

"You were in a heightened state then. Your adrenaline was pumped, and now you're feeling different. It happens sometimes. Take your time. If you need to sit down for a few minutes, go ahead. We're not in a hurry."

"No, it's okay. I'm fine." I didn't want him to think I couldn't handle it. I wasn't sure I could handle it, but I didn't want him to think I couldn't.

"Okay then, look around. Anything appear different to you? Anything seem out of place or missing?"

I glanced around the kitchen. "Do you think maybe they were trying to rob her?"

"I'm not sure what I think yet."

There were little yellow A-frame tents with numbers on them spread throughout the kitchen. One marked the area where Myrtle's body had been, another where the killer left the cast iron skillet on the counter and one marking the glass by the backdoor. "How come there's only one of the markers by the backdoor? Shouldn't there be at least two?"

"Why do you say that?" Dylan asked. "Maybe the big cities use one for each piece of glass, but out here, we count the glass as one item."

"I'm not talking about the glass. I'm talking about the caked mud. Wouldn't that be considered separate evidence?"

"What mud?"

"The mud that was on the floor." I stared down at the worn linoleum and pointed as I walked back to where I'd found Myrtle's body. "In fact, the mud went all the way to here." I turned around and headed toward the back hallway and the den. "And if I remember correctly, I noticed a bit of it in the hallway here, too. Why aren't there markers here?"

Dylan raised an eyebrow. "We didn't find any mud."

I jabbed my finger repeatedly at the linoleum. "Really? There was caked mud on the floor. Pieces of it. Like it had come out of the crack of someone's shoe." I stared at the floor again and then raised my eyes slowly up to his. "Oh my gosh. He was still here. The killer was still in the house when I found Myrtle." I leaned against the kitchen counter and forced myself to breathe in slow, deep breaths. I didn't want to hyperventilate. The last time I did that in Dylan's presence was the night he broke up with me, and there was no way I'd ever let him see me do that again.

"You okay?"

I nodded but kept focused on my breathing. "Fine." I waved my hand because I couldn't say much else. I wobbled a bit against the counter.

He lightly gripped my shoulders with his hands, steadying me better than I could myself. I wanted to push his hands away. I would have told him to not touch me, but in that moment all that mattered was that I could have been killed by the same person that killed my client. "Lil, the killer couldn't have still been here. Myrtle's body is in rigor. Her body temperature is the same as the house, and it takes hours for that to happen."

I breathed in one last deep breath and felt calm enough to speak an entire sentence. For the most part, at least. "I don't understand."

"Granted, it's hot as blazes in here, but still." He moved away from me and then back again but toward me but not close enough to touch. "A body cools in death. Drops about a degree and a half an hour, give or take, until it hits room temperature." He showed me a page on his little note pad. "Coroner took Myrtle's temperature—trust me, you don't want to know how—and checked it against the thermostat. Based on the rough math, she'd already been dead about nine hours by the time you got here. That's just an estimate of course. We'll know more once the autopsy is done. But that means there's no way the killer was here with you."

Unless he came back.

"But there was mud on the floor Dylan. I swear I saw it."

"People don't realize how stressful it is to see a dead body. That's why we question witnesses more than once. Things come up. Things change. You'll remember things differently, or you'll remember things later that you didn't remember now. Maybe you're misplacing the mud from another memory.

Happens all the time in these kinds of situations."

"I guess." Dylan was the expert, so he was probably right. Finding Myrtle dead was stressful, and who knows what kind of tricks my mind could play on me in that kind of situation. Ask me about selling a house, and I was the expert. Ask me about murder and my knowledge was limited to fictional crime solving from prime-time TV. Gosh, Belle was right. I really did need a hobby.

"How much home improvement work did you have Myrtle doing around the house?" he asked.

"None, actually. Like I said, she's planning, or she planned to sell the house to a multi-unit builder, not a single family. I suggested she keep the main lawn area and the house tidy, but no changes. Why do you ask?"

"The attic's tore up pretty bad. Wasn't sure what the point of that was for the home sale."

"The attic?"

He nodded. "Holes in the drywall and the floor's pulled up in spots. From the fresh drywall dust everywhere, looks like it's new work. Figured you're the one that told her to do it."

"Can I take a look?"

He flicked his head toward the stairs. "Come on. I'll show you."

I appreciated that. Even though the killer was obviously not in the house at that moment, I didn't feel comfortable going to the attic alone.

Dylan was right. The entire attic was in shambles. The walls had holes randomly punched throughout them, and the old wood floor was pulled up in various spots, no rhyme or reason to any of it whatsoever.

I had to climb over books, boxes, tools, and all sorts of odds and ends tossed around on the ground from the shelves and maybe the drawers of the cabinets and dressers just to get around the crowded, tight room. If I had any sort of claustrophobia, it would have sent me into a panic attack, but thankfully, I didn't. "Dylan, I didn't tell her to do this, and it wasn't like this the other day, I swear." I carefully maneuvered through the small, stuffy room. "I was just here. In fact, Myrtle had asked me to take a look up here and make sure the door was locked. She didn't want anyone coming up here when viewing the property. Said there were some family things she didn't want disturbed. I told her she wouldn't have to worry about it, but she insisted."

"You sure about that?"

I climbed back down the stairs. "Yes, Sheriff Roberts, I am sure."

That annoying adorable twitch thing at the corner of his mouth started again. "What day were you up here?"

"Thursday."

"And as far as you know, Myrtle didn't have any plans to alter this room in any way?"

"She told me to lock the door so she could keep people out, Dylan. She was eighty-five-years-old. You think she was going to come up here and do a remodel herself? No, she had no plans to remodel this room."

He nodded and headed toward the front of the house.

"Why would someone do this? Do you really think it was Jesse?" I hit him with a list of questions a mile long. By the time we got to the front door, I could tell I'd worn him out. "Maybe you're right." I kind of talked more to myself than to my ex-boyfriend. "Maybe there's something of value to Jesse up here, and he wanted it, so he killed her and came looking for it after? Or maybe he came looking for it before he killed her and couldn't find it, so he killed her because she wouldn't tell him where it was?"

He stepped outside and rubbed his short, cropped blond hair before putting his hat back on. "Is there anything else you can tell me?"

I cocked my head to the right and shook it. "You didn't hear a thing I said, did you?"

"Sure, I did."

'Liar. You're doing exactly what you did when we dated."

His head flinched back ever so slightly. "I'm what?"

"You acted like you listened then, but you didn't, and you're doing the same thing now."

"I did listen, both then and now."

"Fine. Then answer my questions."

"Which ones?"

"All of them. Any of them."

He couldn't.

"You didn't hear any of them."

"I'm sorry." He sighed. "I don't have any answers at the moment anyway, Lil. What I do have is more questions for you."

I tensed my jaw, focusing hard on letting the past stay where it belonged for the moment so I could focus on poor Myrtle Redbecker. "Okay, go ahead."

"You didn't notice anything before you went inside? Maybe you heard something you didn't realize before?"

I replayed the events back in my head. "I don't think so. But you know, Sonny Waddell mentioned he came by to see Myrtle last night. He gave me the impression they had words. Maybe you should talk to him."

"Did he say what time he came by?"

I shook my head. "But I talked to her at about 4:30, so she was alive then."

He nodded. "Anything else?"

"Not that I can think of."

He held onto the brim of his hat with his thumb and forefinger and tipped it toward me. "Thank you, Lilybit."

"You know I hate that."

His mouth twitched. "I know."

That twitch. Lord, that twitch. It would be the death of me.

* * *

On my way to the office I stopped at Millie's Coffee and Cakes to grab an iced vanilla coffee and one of Millie's famous raspberry lemon scones to go. I ordered a sweet tea and blueberry scone for Belle also. I went through the motions of my normal day even though Myrtle's death left me a bit shell shocked and out of sorts. I figured it was the best way to return to normal.

Millie handed me the change from my twenty-dollar bill. "Can you believe it?" She shook her head. "Myrtle Redbecker dead. Bless Patsy, I knew that old coot would kick the bucket, but I never thought someone would kill her."

Word traveled fast in a small town.

"It's sad, I know. No one deserves to die like that."

"It's awful, just awful." She closed her register and leaned toward me. "I'm not one for spreading gossip, but I hear Sheriff Roberts already has her killer, that nephew of hers. That poor boy, he just ain't been the same since his family passed. And I heard he's in debt something fierce. Bad business deal or something like that. Needs the money from the sale of the property to keep his garage now, I hear."

"Now Millie, don't you go assuming something without knowing the facts. You know what my momma always said about that." I winked without saying exactly what my momma always said about that, thanked her for the food and headed to the office.

I figured I'd let that one sit with Millie a bit. Sometimes the small town gossip got on my nerves. Having been the center of it once, I had a little empathy for Jesse Pickett. I wasn't sure if he killed his aunt, though I strongly suspected he did, but I couldn't participate in throwing him under the bus without any real evidence against him.

The drive to my office was so short I could have walked, but I liked having my car a few steps from our store front location, and within eyesight of our office window. I handed Belle her tea and scone and plunked myself into my desk chair, the events of the morning already catching up with me, and it wasn't even afternoon. My stomach ached, but not because I needed sustenance, because I'd found my client dead from a head wound and had a horrible feeling her only living relative was the person that killed her. I needed to focus on work so I didn't focus on Myrtle's death.

"Why are you even here?" she asked. "If ever you need a day off, it's today." She bit into her scone and swallowed it down with a sweet tea chaser. "I can handle things here."

"I know, but I've got the Wilkinson property paperwork to get ready, and that new relocation company sent me their presentation a week ago, and I still haven't watched it yet. I'm feeling a bit overwhelmed."

"That can all wait. Maybe you need to go take a spin class to destress. Pull those blonde curls up into a ponytail and go hop on a bike. It'll make you feel better."

Spin classes were my go-to exercise and destressing avenue of choice, and Belle knew that. She also knew I had a slight addiction to staying in shape ever since I'd learned most of the women in my family ended up with first Type 1 and then Type 2 diabetes. I'd made a conscious decision to eat fairly well and exercise often hoping to not end up like the rest of my family. I knew I'd end up exercising soon, but something about the situation with Myrtle Redbecker had my brain working on overdrive. "I'll go later." I took a bite of my scone, too, forgetting, at least momentarily, about the risk of diabetes. "Something's not right."

"Goodness, don't go telling Millie that. The last time someone complained about her scones she banned him from the store for life. Remember that?"

I laughed. "Caroline Chastain's great grandpa. We had to bring him scones every morning on our way to school. Poor guy."

Belle leaned back in her chair and laughed too. "I know. He even brought her flowers to apologize, but she wouldn't even let him inside. Locked the door and told him he could put the flowers where the sun didn't shine."

"Obviously he didn't know that no one should ever mess with a woman and her scone recipe." I took another bite of the creamy but dry treat. "And really, what is there to complain about anyway?"

"Absolutely nothing."

I finished chewing. "That's not what I'm talking about though. I'm talking about Myrtle. Dylan thinks Jesse killed her, but I'm not sure I agree. You were right by the way."

"About what?"

"There was someone in the house when I got there. I think they left between the time I arrived and called the police."

She straightened in her chair. "Oh my gosh. You could have been killed. Did you tell Dylan?"

"I did. He thinks I'm just stressed because of the whole situation." I filled her in on the details.

"How long did it take Dylan to get there after you called 9-1-1?"

"Not long. Maybe a few minutes. Five at the most."

"Well, he is the one with training in this kind of thing." She grabbed a hair clip from the collar of her shirt, twisted her long, straight black hair into a bun and clipped it on the top of her head. I envied the neatness of her stick straight hair.

"You don't have to remind me about that." The amount of baggage I carried because of Dylan's decision to become law enforcement could fill a land fill. I wasn't prepared to go there and dig any of it up any time soon. I picked a pen out of the cup on my desk and twirled it in my hand. "Do you think Dylan's right? About Jesse?"

"I'm leaning that way. Maybe he heard you yelling for Myrtle, and he ran out when you called 9-1-1." She stared at out our office window onto the town's main street. "Maybe It's Sonny Waddell. He said he was there the night before, remember?"

"Millie said she heard Jesse Pickett got involved with some bad business deal and is in a lot of debt because of it. Apparently, he might lose the garage over it. She thinks it's him, too. Poor guy's been proven guilty before he's even gone to trial."

"He's never been the same since losing his family."

"That's what Millie said." My thoughts kept going back to the attic. What could be up there that Jesse, or even Sonny Waddell might want that would be worth killing Myrtle Redbecker over? "I saw what's in that attic, and there's nothing of any real monetary value up there. Yeah, Myrtle said there's some family things she didn't want anyone to touch, but all that's up there is a bunch of photos and stuff like that. She actually asked me to make sure a few of the boxes were removed and attended to if something happened to her. Said there's a letter at the bank in her safety deposit box if the need arises that'll tell me what to do with some of the items."

"One man's trash is another man's treasure."

"You watch too many home improvement shows."

"I'm a realtor. Of course, I do."

I tapped the pen on my desk. "There's something going on. I don't know what, but I don't think we can sell that property until we figure it out." I kept tapping the pen on my desk. Tap. Tap. Tap.

"If you don't stop that there's going to be another murder."

"Stop what?"

"The tapping with the darn pen. Please, go work out. When you get like this, you drive everyone around you crazy. Expend that energy before I stick that pen where the sun don't shine."

"Oh, my." I grabbed my gym back from under my desk. "Testy this morning, aren't you?"

"If your best friend was Type A, you'd go crazy from all the tapping too, trust me."

I tapped the pen on the desk a few more times, and Belle threw a pad of paper at me.

"Get out of here," she yelled, smiling the entire time.

I ran out laughing.

An hour and a half and a full-throttle spin class later, my stress level lessened, but I hadn't changed my mind. We still couldn't finalize the sale of Myrtle Redbecker's property without figuring out who killed her.

Chapter Two

Getting answers about families in small towns wasn't all that tough. Everyone knew something about everyone, and they all had an opinion about it, too. The tough part was determining fact from gossip and truth from lies, so I decided to just ask questions first and worry about separating the answers later.

In college, I'd learned to attack every business situation with a plan, and I'd made that a practice in most areas of my life, too. Belle swore I did that with dating too, and that I needed more spontaneity in my life, but I had a very specific list of requirements for my special someone, and a plan of when I'd start the process of finding him, and I had no intentions of changing that plan. Spontaneity caused heartache; I knew that from personal experience. Personal experience I had no intention of repeating ever again.

I didn't have a detailed plan to figure out what the story was behind Myrtle's murder, but I wasn't flying by the seat of my pants, either. I had a general idea of what to do—ask questions and go from there. Sometimes that was what I did when securing a client, too. I asked questions, a lot of questions, and eventually I'd hit on something that clicked, and I made the sale.

I had two possible suspects with at least one potential motive and something just on the other side of a motive, but it was better than nothing, so I went with it. The obvious, Myrtle's nephew Jesse, and the not so obvious, her neighbor, Sonny Waddell. The motives weren't all that solid, if Sonny even had one, but digging a little deeper into both stories wouldn't hurt.

I opted to kill two birds with one stone and headed over to Odell Luna's house. I plugged my nose as I got out of my car, but that didn't do me a whole lot of good. The ammonia scent hit me so hard anyway, I tasted it. Myrtle

Redbecker's murder was tops on my list, but I definitely needed to address the chickens. Someone had to.

I kept my nose plugged and knocked on his door. He acknowledged my knock with a cranky holler of, "I'm coming, quit your banging."

I'd only knocked twice.

"What do you want?" When he finally made eye contact, he blushed. "Oh, Lily Sprayberry." He pushed his greasy gray combover that had dropped over his left eye, to the side. "Nice to see you."

"Nice to see you too, Mr. Luna. May I come in?"

He straightened the bottom of his no longer white undershirt. "I reckon so, though I don't got nothing for you to drink but beer and water. You want one of those?"

I waved my hand. "No, thank you. I'm fine. I'd just like to talk with you about Mrs. Redbecker's property if you don't mind." I sat on his worn green and yellow couch. His house smelled as bad inside as it did outside.

"Don't mind one bit. Terrible thing to happen to her. Myrtle wasn't the sweetest berry on the branch, but me and her, we got along all right. Hate to see her go that way."

He shook his head. "Eighty-five years and then hit over the head with your cast iron skillet."

"It's terrible, I know. I overheard you talking with Sonny Waddell earlier. You mentioned something about not having to worry about Myrtle selling the property now because Jesse would get it. That got Sonny's tail up, and I'm wondering what he meant when he said neither Jesse or his aunt would be getting his property. I'm not aware of Myrtle trying to purchase Sonny's property. Do you know what he was talking about?"

Odell unearthed a bottle of moonshine from his TV cabinet and poured some into a paper cup. He offered me a sip, but I kindly declined. I'd tried the stuff in high school and after a hangover the size of the state of Texas, decided alcohol wasn't my thing. I hadn't had a sip of the stuff since.

"Myrtle didn't tell you about the property dispute? I'd have thought you'd be the first to know considering you're the real estate agent of record and all."

"No, she didn't. I'd love for you to explain it to me. If you don't mind, of course."

He chugged the rest of his drink and poured himself another cup full. "'Course. Looks like there's a bit of a disagreement over part of the land. Sonny claims it's his, but Myrtle had a different opinion. Now that she's gone and Jesse's getting the house, he'll have to deal with him over it."

"Do you know what section of land Sonny thinks is his?"

He nodded and wiggled his finger for me to follow him outside. "See that corner over there? The one next to that big River Birch? On the left of the tree, that's what everyone's always figured was the dividing line, but Sonny claims it ain't. Says it's actually on the other side of the tree."

I knew nothing about the property line issue and assumed it was because Myrtle believed there wasn't one. "Has he had survey done?"

He nodded. "You know who used to work for the county appraiser's office, right?"

"Wilbur Redbecker."

"Sonny thinks he rigged the property lines in his favor. Said he doesn't care what the survey says, he knows his land and he ain't sellin' it to nobody, and he's tired of letting that old biddy tell him what to do with it, too." His cheeks turned a touch pink. "Excuse me. Those were his words, not mine. I don't speak ill of the dead."

I patted his shoulder. "It's okay Odell. I understand." We weren't close enough to the area to get a good view of the land, and I had no idea how far Sonny claimed it extended anyway. "About how big of a section of land are we talking about?"

Odell tapped his chin. "Supposed to stretch all the way to the end of the property, so I'd guess about a couple acres when it's all said and done. You measure it out right though, and it'll come out different. Math wasn't never my strong point."

"Mine either. I'll have to check with the tax assessor and see how they'd measure that."

Junior appeared from the back side of Myrtle's house with his shovel in hand. Jesse followed closely behind him, his voice loud enough for the neighbors a mile down the road to hear.

"I told you to leave my property alone, Junior, and I meant it. I know what you're doing, and the two of you need to stay out of my business."

Junior's voice was quiet enough that I had to hone in my attention to hear him. "I don't know what you're talking about, Jesse. Miss Sprayberry gave me the go-ahead to keep working. You got a problem with that, you talk to her. I don't answer to you."

Jesse glanced our way and noticed us staring at him. I gave a gentle wave and he marched off toward the front of the house and disappeared.

Jesse wasn't in jail, so I assumed Dylan's questioning led him to believe he was innocent.

We headed back inside. "You think Jesse'll hand over Sonny's part of the property?"

"Jesse isn't getting the property, Odell. Myrtle has three offers on it, and she'd decided over the weekend. That's why I was there this morning, to discuss to her decision."

"But she's dead now, so don't the property go to Jesse?"

"Unfortunately, no. In the event of her death, Myrtle had the property put into a trust and instructed the trust to work with me to complete the sale. She was adamant the property be sold and not given to her nephew."

"Well I'll be. She went and did it, didn't she?"

"I don't understand."

"She always said she wasn't gonna let that boy get none of her money, even the hidden stuff. Said she'd rather see it go to strangers than that good for nothing boy."

"Hidden stuff?"

"She didn't tell you about that?"

I shook my head.

Odell laughed, a hearty, warm belly laugh. "Lord that woman. If you didn't like her, you had to respect her. She was a tough one, that Myrtle." He kicked a roach across his kitchen floor, and I shivered. "You know Jesse's her great-nephew, not her nephew, right?"

"Born and raised here, Odell. There's not much I don't know." Except about Myrtle's hidden money, obviously.

"Well, I ain't saying this is fact or nothing, but what I know is Myrtle's pawpaw told her and her brother Buford, Jesse's own pawpaw—" he paused. "You following me?"

I nodded.

"He told them there's money hidden somewhere on the property. Just didn't tell them where. Said it could be in the house or the land, but it was their job to figure it out." He dug into the pocket of his baggy trousers, pulled out a canister of tobacco chew, picked some from it and stuffed it down behind his lower lip. I no longer wondered why his teeth were stained yellow, not that I didn't already know anyway. "Buford could never find it nowhere, and the old fart kicked the bucket before he could get anything more out of him. But Myrtle? She claimed she knew where it was, and she never would tell her brother. He died, but not before he made his son promise to find that money 'fore his sister did. Only he got himself killed in that car crash before he did, too. Jesse's been trying to find it ever since."

I'd heard a lot of stories in my short twenty-six years, but that was a new one. "You think it's true?"

"Don't think much about it either way, but if I had to guess, I'd say yup. Ain't easy making up something like that."

"You think Sonny knows the story?"

"'Course he does. Don't think he'd be pitching such a fit if he didn't."

I thought out loud. "Maybe he thinks the money is buried on his part of the land." I straightened my shoulders. "And since Wilbur worked for the county assessor…"

He spit the chew into his empty cup. "Now you're getting it."

I stood. "Thanks, Odell. I really appreciate you talking with me." I rushed toward the front door.

Odell shuffled behind me. "Anytime, Lilybit. Anytime."

"Oh, one more thing." I pulled out my phone. "Do you have a piece of paper and a pencil?"

He hobbled back to his kitchen and returned with both items.

I jotted down a name and phone number from my phone address book. "Please give this man a call. He can come and clean out your chicken coop. The smell is horrible, and it's not good for the chickens."

His head flinched backward. "Those chickens smell? I darn knew my hearing was out a kilter, but I didn't know my nose was, too." He took the paper from me and set it on the table near his front door. "I'll get on out there and get to cleaning it up myself. I may be old, but I'm still capable of cleaning out a chicken coop. 'Course I can't smell no more, but I didn't know that till you pointed it out."

I shrugged and raised the volume of my voice a touch. "At least now you do."

He smiled and waved as I headed to my car and then hollered to me, "Oh, by the way, if them builders decide they want to talk to me, I might could give them a bit of time to listen."

"I gotcha, Odell," I hollered back.

The county assessor's office was a short drive away, and I made it there in less than fifteen minutes. I requested a copy of the map for Myrtle's property and the three surrounding plots. I also requested any and all previous filings, surveys, updates and disputes on the properties. I wasn't a map expert, but I wanted to find out approximately how much land Sonny might gain if he could prove it was his.

I was told it would take three to five days for the maps, but if I paid twenty-five dollars, I could get them in twenty-four hours, so I tossed the woman my debit card figuring I'd add it to Myrtle's bill. If I didn't do my due diligence for the sale, it could come back to bite the new owners in the butt and damage my reputation, and I didn't want that.

I headed back to work, but not before stopping off at Millie's again for another bite to go.

I stood in front of her pastry counter admiring the artwork she called baked goods. Her mini muffins came in all sorts of flavors, my favorite being banana nut. I'd tried to convince her to give me the recipe, but she refused. Millie believed her recipes were a gift from the good Lord above, as she'd said, and if she shared them with the world, she'd end up living in a box on the side of Buford Highway in Atlanta. I tried to tell her she might end up with a café in Buckhead, but she didn't want that, so her secret recipes stayed secret.

She'd just made a fresh batch of something that included apples and cinnamon. The aroma filling the café brought me back to winters past and nights filled with hot apple cider as I sat on the front porch swing and listened to my father tell ghost stories.

The memory tugged at my heartstrings. Sometimes I hated that I was twenty-six-years-old and wanted my parents close by. I knew other people my age wanted to be away from their parents. They wanted to move from their families, from their home towns, and see the world, but my world was Bramblett County Georgia, and that suited me just fine.

"Well, lookie here. Twice in one day. You must be making the big bucks these days," Millie said.

"Don't I wish. I'd just rather be broke with a tummy full of your fabulous food than living month to month with a peanut butter and jelly sandwich made by yours truly."

She pressed her palm to her chest. "Well, now ain't that the sweetest thing?"

I wasn't exaggerating either. "What is that heavenly smell?"

"It's my new apple and cinnamon scone. I'm trying something a little different. Would you like a sample?"

"Anyone that would turn down a sample of something you've made should be sent straight to the looney bin, Millie."

"Your momma raised you right." She hollered to the back and out came a sample of the new scone.

I inhaled the bite sized piece of ecstasy like it was the last food on earth. "Oh, my stars, I just died and went to scone heaven. Millie, that is wonderful. Truly, you've outdone yourself this time."

Her skinned glowed a flushed pink. "Why thank you, Lilybit. Your order is on me today."

I didn't argue. It wouldn't have done me any good anyway. What Millie said in her own café was the law, and I'd learned that a long time ago. I ordered my favorite sandwich with fresh fruit and a bag of her homemade kettle chips and chatted her up while she totaled out my bill. "Have you heard the story about the buried money over at Myrtle's?"

"'Course I have. Everyone knows that story."

"Do you think there's any truth to it?"

"I sure do. Word is Boone Picket, Myrtle's pawpaw, wasn't one for lying, so if he said there's money somewhere on the Redbecker's property or wherever he claimed it is, then it's there."

"Have you heard where it might be?"

"There's been talk over the years, but Myrtle wouldn't let no one check. Kept everyone away with a loaded shotgun 'cept for the last few years when those meal delivery people started bringing her food." Her kitchen girl came out with my meal and Millie bagged it for me. "She'd probably have shot them, too, if they didn't bring the right meal. That woman was as mean as the day is long."

She handed me my bag. "She wasn't all that bad, though she did complain sometimes at our Monday meetings. She would be upset if the food wasn't delivered on time the night before because it would ruin her sleep and daily constitutional schedule."

"A woman my age can understand that. And she liked you 'cause you were doing something for her. You crossed that woman, she'd draw a big X on your head and reserve a bullet just for you."

Millie's gossip bordered on storytelling but saying my old lady client would shoot someone was a bit extreme. I let it go though, because exaggerated information was better than no information. "Well, I'm lucky she liked me then." I thanked her for the meal and headed back to the office.

I opened the sandwich in the car and finished it quickly. I hadn't realized it, but I was famished. When I passed my office I'd already downed most of the bag of chips, too. I'd made the decision to skip the office entirely and head over to Jesse's work as I stuffed the sandwich in my mouth. I wasn't quite sure what I would say to him but figured giving him my condolences would be a good place to start.

Even though the big double garage doors to his auto shop sat open, the garage still smelled like old oil and car exhaust. Two cars sat up on raised jacks, one a beat up Chevy of some sort—I only knew by the brand symbol—and the other and old Ford Mustang. Jesse lay under the Chevy.

"Knock, knock," I said. I didn't want to surprise him.

He slid out from under the car, a look of irritation on his face. "Oh, hey." He wiped his forehead with the palm of his hand and left a line of oil across it.

I shifted my weight from one foot to another. "I just wanted to come by and you know, tell you I'm sorry about your aunt."

He stood and wiped the grease from his hands onto a blue cloth. "You found her, right?"

I nodded.

"Your boyfriend won't even let me in the house. Said it's a crime scene, but that's my family's home. I need to know what happened there."

He wanted to know if the money had been found. "He's my ex-boyfriend. I don't really know what happened. I just went to see your aunt, but she didn't answer the door, so, worried something was wrong, I went in, and when I saw her, I called 9-1-1 right away."

"The property belongs to me now. I know you got all that legal stuff that says it don't, but I'm her last kin, and it should come to me. I don't want you messing around there no more."

"Those decisions have already been made, Jesse. You'll have to talk to an attorney if you'd like them changed."

"I can't afford no attorney. I talked to my aunt last night. Told her it was wrong, what she did. Don't matter that we don't get along. We're still family. That house belonged to my great pawpaw. Don't seem to matter if she thought I should get it or not."

"You saw her last night?"

He nodded. "Went there 'fore dark. Tried to get her to change her mind, but she said the deal was already done. Said she'd already got a buyer. That true?"

"Sort of. There are three builders interested in the property. They've all placed bids. I was meeting with Myrtle this morning so she could tell me which bid she'd decided on, but now it's up to the trust to decide."

"Won't be a single one of them if I have anything to say about it." He tossed the cloth onto his work bench. "And you need to keep Junior off that land. I don't care what my aunt hired him to do, that ain't the reason he's there, Lily, and I know it."

Everyone in town knew Jesse and Junior were best friends growing up, but something happened after Jesse's parents died, and the two despised each other. Their parting hadn't been a peaceful one, either. They flat out hated each other, and everyone in town knew it.

"Jesse, I know you don't like Junior, but Myrtle asked him to do some tree work and to keep the main lawn area maintained. If the trust continues to allow him to work on the—"

"I'm telling you, I know what he's doing, and if you know what's good for you, you'll keep him away. You understand?" His voice echoed throughout the garage.

Was he saying Junior was looking for the hidden money?

I stepped back. "Okay, well, I…I just wanted to come by and tell you I'm sorry for your loss."

He slammed a handful of assorted tools down onto his bench without offering me another acknowledgement as I retreated from his garage.

I got in my car and hightailed it out of there. I drove around a bit trying to put the pieces of the puzzle together. Why didn't Myrtle want her nephew to have the property? What kind of falling out could an aunt and her great-nephew have? And if Junior thought he could find the cash, did he really think finders keepers would hold up in court? Did Sonny think the money was buried somewhere on land he thought belonged to his family? And if it was, would the whole possession was nine-tenths of the law thing be true? My legal experience from TV did nothing for me, and it frustrated me to no end.

I headed back home thinking I would check emails and follow up with work there instead of the office. Five minutes into the drive, Dylan pulled me over.

"License and registration, please."

"You're kidding, right?"

He offered me that slight twitch and my insides melted. "What're you doing on this side of town?"

"Not that it's any of your business, but I had some things to attend to." I inhaled the freshness of his soapy smell and caught myself as my mouth curved upward. The last thing I needed was for my ex-boyfriend to see me smiling like a school girl while pulling me over. He'd probably think I was flirting with him.

He rested his forearms on my opened window. "Those things include talking to Jesse Pickett?"

"Are you following me?"

"It's my duty to make sure the citizens of this community remain safe, ma'am."

Gosh, he sure was cute. I hated him for it. Almost. I almost hated him for it. "So, wouldn't that be more like stalking then? Isn't that against the law, Sheriff?"

"As I said, it's my duty to protect the citizens of this county, ma'am."

I tried hard not to laugh, but despite my efforts, I giggled. "I might have stopped by. It's been a while since I've had my car serviced."

He pulled a little spiral note pad from his front pocket, flipped it open and then pretended to take notes with his finger. "You're telling me you went there to have your car checked?"

"I'm saying it's been a while since I've had my car serviced." That wasn't a lie. It wasn't an answer to his question either, but it wasn't a lie.

He grunted something under his breath and then closed the note pad and stuffed it back into the pocket.

"I'm sorry, can you repeat that?"

He smirked. "Did you discuss my case with him?"

"I expressed my condolences for the loss of his aunt, yes."

"Anything else?"

"No, not really."

He nodded. "Okay. Might I remind you, this is an active investigation, and I'd appreciate it if you'd keep the things we discussed to yourself, and I think it's best you stay away from anything having to do with the case for the time being."

"Yes, sir, Sheriff."

He tipped his hat to me. "Thank you, ma'am."

I expected him to turn and leave, but he didn't, so I just sat there, all awkward and nervous, with my palms sweating. I leaned forward a bit to hide the fact that I needed to rub them on my jeans. Every time my nerves got the best of me, my palms sweat. Not that Dylan would remember that, but just in case…

"Where you headed now?"

"Again, not that it's any of your business, but I'm going home."

He glanced into the back of my car. "No workout bag? You give up those cycling classes?"

Was he actually stalking me? How did he know I took spin classes? "They're called spin, and how do you even know I take them? Are you stalking me now or something?"

He pointed to the sticker on my back window. "Life Fitness and Spin Studio preferred parking sticker, and you always had a bag in your car back when we, you know. So, I just assumed."

I blushed. "Oh, I forgot about the sticker."

He busied himself by adjusting the police radio on his shirt collar. "I just wondered if you had any plans for this evening. I'm off in an hour and thought maybe we could grab dinner later." He paused. "To, you know, go over any questions you might have about the case."

Had my ex just asked me out on a date? "I uh, I can't. I'm sorry. I have plans. A date. Yeah, I have a date." I'd just lied like a dog on a rug. I glanced down at my lap. I couldn't make eye contact when I lied to someone, which was probably why I rarely did it. If Dylan remembered anything about me, he'd remember that. He would tease me about it all the time, how I'd never lie to my parents about why I got home late, or why I wasn't where I said I'd be. He thought it was cute, my inability to be dishonest, and I thought I was a horrible person if I lied.

He coughed, and I had to glance up at him. He knew. I'd been busted, but I didn't fess up. I just went with it.

His eyes sparkled, and I thought he was going to smile, but he went with it, too. "Oh, okay. We can talk about the case another time then."

"Yeah, uh…sure. Another time."

He turned to leave and then flipped back around. "I meant what I said though, Lilybit. Stay away from Jesse Pickett."

* * *

"You told him what?" Belle laughed into her phone. "You haven't had a date since he broke up with you."

"That's not true."

"Friends taking you to sorority formals don't count."

"They do so, and I've had other dates."

"Oh yeah? Name one."

My mind blanked.

"Told you."

"I've been busy. I haven't really had a chance to focus on dating."

"For seven years?"

I bit my lip.

"All you've ever wanted was Dylan, and he's been back for almost a year now, and finally asks you out, and you turn him down with a lie? What were you thinking?"

"I don't know. I wasn't really. I just kind of blurted it out."

"Well, next time stuff a sock in it."

"Don't be salty with me." I pulled up to my little green one-story bungalow with its covered front porch that always brought a smile to my face every time I saw it and shut off my car. I didn't notice my side door was slightly ajar until after I closed and locked my car door. "Hey, let me call you back."

Belle continued to lay into me about lying to Dylan, but I disconnected our call. I was certain I'd shut and locked that door when I'd left that morning, but so much had happened I could have been wrong. I entered my kitchen with caution, holding my bag close to my chest, as if that would protect me somehow. Nothing seemed out of place, I didn't smell gas or anything out of the ordinary. Maybe some over ripe oranges in the basket on the table, but nothing like gas or carbon monoxide. I relaxed thinking I'd totally over-reacted and simply forgot to lock my door and dropped my bag on the table when I noticed my cast iron skillet sitting next to it. I hadn't left it there. I hadn't even touched the thing in months. And lying in the skillet was a note that read, *make sure that property don't sell or else.*

I might have been flighty enough to leave my door unlocked, but I certainly hadn't left myself a threatening note, so who did?

Jesse?

I called Dylan right away.

I waited in my car down the street—at his insistence—until he arrived five minutes later. He told me to stay put—which I didn't—and checked my entire house twice before giving me the all clear.

"You never were a good listener, were you?"

"You really can't expect me to stay away from my own house in this kind of situation, can you?"

He nodded. "Actually, I can." He meandered to my stove and played with the knobs.

"I really don't like having people I barely know in my house without me."

He stopped, turned around and stared at me. "People you barely know? Are you talking about the intruder or me?"

"Actually, both."

"So, I'm what, a stranger to you now?"

I glanced down at my floor. "You know what I mean."

"No, actually, I don't." He lifted the note in the skillet by its corner and placed it in the small plastic baggie I'd given him. "But this isn't the time to discuss it." He held the baggie up and waved it my direction. "Care to tell me what this is about?"

I grabbed two bottled waters from the 'fridge and handed him one. "Let's sit on the front porch. It's got a great view of the sun setting. I'll tell a story about some hidden money."

After I told him about the possible hidden money, Dylan rubbed his temples. "I don't know whether to laugh or be angry."

"Laughing seems like the best option."

He agreed. "The people in this town? I swear, sometimes I think they're crazy."

"I know. That's why you left, remember?"

His smile disappeared. "No, Lily. That's not why I left."

I brushed the comment aside. We both knew I was right anyway. "So, what do you think?"

"About the hidden money?"

I nodded.

"I think it's pretty strong motive for murder."

"For who?"

"The butler," he said. "It's obvious he did it. With a butcher's knife. In the library." His mouth did that twitching thing again.

"It could be Sonny Waddell or Jesse, don't you think?"

"Seems to me Jesse's got a lot more invested in the loss of the property than a neighbor." He scratched his forehead. "But Sonny neglected to mention any of this when I interviewed him, so I'm going to have to talk to him again." He flipped his hat in his hands. "Either way, I'll find the person who did this, Lil. It's what I'm trained to do."

I knew all about that training and a big part of me hated it. "Was it worth it?"

His hands stilled. "What?"

Dylan had big dreams of a football scholarship at the University of Georgia and then going pro for the NFL. Those dreams died when he blew out his right knee his last year of high school, my sophomore year. He still went to UGA, and we stayed together, but things ended my freshman year at Georgia when he decided to drop out of college and enter the Atlanta Police Academy.

He wanted the big city life, and I wanted the security and familiarity of my small town.

"Leaving. Was it worth it?" I didn't make eye contact with him. Instead, I watched the sky fade from yellow to a golden orange as the sun slowly began to set behind the trees. "You said you'd never come back, and now here you are, our sheriff, by special election and all."

He twisted to face me. "Lil, look at me, please."

I wasn't sure I could.

"I want to talk to you about this, and once this case is solved, I will. It's important to me, and I know it's important to you. Can we just put it on hold for now? Please?"

I finally conjured up the nerve to look him in the eye. "You should go. I have a date to get ready for." I stood and walked back to the kitchen. Dylan followed.

The tension between us filled the small room. Dylan felt it, too, and changed the subject. "I'll make sure to have one of the guys keep a look out on your house for now, but if anything out of the ordinary happens, give me a call, okay?"

I nodded and opened the side door for him.

As I closed the door behind him he stopped it with his hand and said, "I never meant to hurt you, Little Bean."

The use of his private nickname for me nearly shattered my heart to pieces all over again.

CHAPTER THREE

"Who do you think left the note?" Belle asked.

After Dylan left, I packed up a few things and dragged them to Belle's place. My safe little bungalow suddenly felt stuffy and scary, and I knew I wouldn't sleep if I stayed there alone overnight. A good night's sleep and a healthy breakfast in the morning and I'd be back to one hundred percent again and back in my own home. Maybe part of the reason I'd left was because I didn't want to be alone with my hurting heart, but I wasn't ready to admit that to myself, or to Belle. She once told me denial was my shield, but I denied that then and still did.

"The killer." I stuffed a handful of popcorn into my mouth, the salty, buttery flavor attacking the feel-good sensors in my brain. "It can't be anyone else."

She flung a kernel at me and hit me smack dab on the forehead. "And do you still think Jesse didn't do it?"

"After talking to him earlier and seeing that note in my cast iron skillet..." I tossed a few more kernels into my mouth. "...I've pretty much changed my mind."

She agreed.

"He told me he went to Myrtle's yesterday, too."

"Really? That's weird."

"What do you mean?"

"Maybe it's me, but if I'd killed someone, the last thing I'd do is tell someone I'd gone there the day I killed the person." She swallowed back half her glass of Coke. "Then again, I wouldn't be in that situation in the first place."

"Of course, you wouldn't."

"Because they'd never find the body."

"Exactly."

We both laughed.

"You're right though, that does seem a little odd, but a lot of times people don't think about what they're saying, and they just blurt stuff out."

"Kind of like you lying to Dylan about having a date?"

"Can we discuss one topic at a time, please?"

"Of course. Lying. Yes, let's discuss lying. So, why did you lie to Dylan about having a date?"

I pretended she hadn't said anything about that and carried on with our original topic. "Anyway, that's how they catch a lot of the criminals on TV." I realized how silly that sounded when she rolled her eyes. "Maybe he just needs the money so bad he just said it without even realizing it?"

"I think Millie's probably right about him needing the money to keep his shop afloat."

I nodded. "Me too."

"He's always trying those get rich quick schemes, so maybe he got taken or something?"

"Maybe." I tossed a piece of popcorn her direction. She opened her mouth and tried to catch it but missed. "I think tomorrow I'll stop and check on the property and say hello to

Sonny Waddell. Maybe ask him about the survey. See what he has to say."

"You want me to come with you?"

"I appreciate that, but someone's got to run our real estate business, right?"

"I am an excellent office manager."

"Yes, you are. I don't know what we'd do without you."

"You'd still sell a ton of homes since you're the only true realtor in town. You just wouldn't have any fun doing it."

"You're one hundred percent correct."

"May I see your phone, please?"

Suddenly territorial over my cellular device, I covered it on my lap with my hand. "For what?"

She held out her hand. "I'm going to put nude pictures of myself on it. Goodness gracious, do you not trust me?"

I held my phone out. "Of course, I trust you." When she reached to grab it, I yanked it back. "But what do you plan to do with it?"

In some freak speed move I didn't think possible, she snatched it from me. "I'm putting Dylan's contact info into your favorites. If something happens, at least this way you can just tap a button or two and call him instead of having to search through your phone for his number. You may not want to talk to him about your personal relationship, but I don't want anything happening to my bestie, and he's the county sheriff, so deal with it."

"Yes, ma'am." How could I argue with someone that concerned for my safety?

* * *

Before heading to the property, I made a quick stop at the county assessor's office and picked up the property survey maps I'd ordered the day before. I didn't take the time to review them before heading out to Sonny's place.

The old man wasn't happy to see me. "I ain't got nothing to say to you," he said, and slammed the door in my face.

"Mr. Waddell, if you'll just give me a minute, I know you've got some concerns about the property lines, and I'd like to try and help you."

The door opened a crack and he looked fixedly at me. "How do you think you can help me?"

"I don't know exactly." I waved the roll of maps in front of me. "But if you'd talk to me, maybe I can figure it out."

He held the door open, but from the look on his face it was obvious he wasn't all that pleased. "Guess I might could do that."

I held up the rolled surveys. "I'd like you to show me where you believe the property lines should be."

He stared at the maps. "You know that ain't gonna make no difference, right?"

"Maybe, maybe not, but I'd still like to know. If I'm going to sell Myrtle's property, it's important I do my due diligence to make sure I've covered any possible issues regarding the sale, and this is an issue. I'll do what I can to make sure the property lines are correct, whether that's in your favor or not." Sure, I wanted to find out what happened between Myrtle and Sonny, but that wasn't a lie. I needed to do right by my client and the purchaser of the property. My reputation depended on it.

He took the maps from me, moved several piles of stacked newspapers off the oblong coffee table in front of the couch, and rolled the maps out onto the table. The first one was of Odell's property, so he pushed that aside. I took it and rolled it back up. The second was of Myrtle's.

Sonny used his finger to trace a line down his property's side of the map. "See this section right here?" His finger traveled from the back corner of Myrtle's house and all the way down the narrow plot. "If you go about twenty-five feet from the property line, that's where the original line is supposed to be."

"Do you have a copy of your original survey from when you purchased the property? Wouldn't that solve the issue?"

"I didn't purchase the property. It's been in my family since before the Civil War. Ain't no easy way to prove it 'cause of that."

When people settled in Georgia a lot of them just staked a claim on pieces of land and it became theirs. Sonny's family probably did the same. "Is that how Myrtle's family got their land, too?"

"The Pickett's been living here forever, too, but I don't know if they was here 'fore us. See, you ain't asking anything we ain't already tried to find the answers to."

"I understand, but I have to catch up. Why don't you tell me when this property issue all started? Maybe that will help me."

He leaned back into the couch and ran his hand down his long gray beard. "Oh, I'd say maybe fifteen years ago. I was wanting to put up a fence for the missus. She had this inkling to get some goats, but those little boogers like to wander, so I figured I'd put us up a fence. Only when I got to doing it, Myrtle come out and tore me apart. Said I was building it on her property and she'd sue me if I didn't stop." He motioned for me to follow him outside, so I did. "I told her my property went past the other side of those River Birch trees, but she said it stopped on my side of them. I got the survey and it showed the line like she said." He rubbed his beard again. "Don't think it's no coincidence Wilbur Redbecker worked for the county assessor's office."

"How much of the land did you want to fence in?"

"Few acres was all."

"Your land is wider than Myrtle's, correct?"

"Yes, ma'am, but it's the same length. I got about double the acreage, minus the part she stole from me, of course."

"Before you wanted to install the fence, had there ever been any question about the property line?"

He shook his head. "No, ma'am. Never even discussed it."

I assumed Sonny knew the rumors about the money, but I preferred he mention it first.

"Is there any reason Myrtle would want to keep that portion of land? Does it have some kind of special meaning or something?"

"Old Boone Pickett said there's money hidden somewhere either in the house or on the property, but he never said where. I guess Myrtle don't want me getting hold of it."

"But if the property was yours in the first place, why would it even be relative to that old story?"

"'Cause they think the property was theirs from the start, that's why."

That made sense. "Sonny, I overheard you mention to Odell yesterday that you were at Myrtle's last night. Would you mind telling me why?"

His eyes darted to the ground. "I went to talk about her selling her land to one of those developers. I knew that was her plan. One of them come by my house the other day and tried to get me to sell my land to them, too. Said they'd give me top dollar. They want to put up some of those condominiums, they said. I ain't selling my property to no builder, and I don't want no condos next to my land."

I'd suddenly been squished into the space between a rock and a hard place. "Things are changing around here, Sonny. It's called progress."

"Don't mean I have to change with them."

"So, how did the conversation go?"

He glanced down again. "Wasn't good. Myrtle wasn't never no sweetheart, that's for sure. Said the same thing you said. Times are changing and all that. Said I needed to get over myself and change with them."

"Did you talk about the property line issue?"

He nodded. "Said ain't nothing nobody would do about it. What's done was done, and I had to let it go. But I told her I wasn't planning on doing that. Said I'd fight her for my share of the land 'cause it was rightfully mine. Told her I'd die before I let her sell my land."

"Did things escalate between the two of you?"

He looked me right in the eyes. "You think I killed that old coot, don't you? Well, I didn't, and you can ask that meal delivery girl. She'll tell you Myrtle was alive when I left her. She saw me." He brushed past the coffee table, whipped the survey maps from it, and threw them at me. "Now I think I've given you all the time I can. Don't need nobody accusing me of killing Myrtle Redbecker like that. Go on now, get outta my house."

"I wasn't accusing you of killing Myrtle, Sonny, but I think you—"

He cut me off. "Go on, get out." He crowded behind me so I couldn't turn around and face him and made sure he stayed that way all the way to my car. I didn't push back. If he did kill my client, the last thing I needed to do was upset him more.

I pulled out of his lot and drove toward town, asking Siri to call Dylan on the way. He answered on the first ring. "Everything okay?"

"Everything's fine. I'm curious. Have you spoken to Sonny Waddell yet?"

"Briefly, but I'm headed to his place now. Why?"

Yikes. "Just wondering. I mentioned that I overheard him say he'd been to Myrtle's on Sunday night, right?"

"Yes."

"Okay, that's it. Just following up."

"Lily."

"Yeah?"

"What's going on?"

I tapped on the phone. "Hello? Dylan? Are you there?" I shook my cell—like he could actually see the thing. "Hello? I think I lost you. Darn it." I hit the red phone handle icon to end the call and told myself I'd apologize later. I wanted to stop by the community center on my way to the office and find out who did the meal delivery for Myrtle's area on Sunday evening. If Dylan was on his way to Sonny's place, it was safe to assume he'd end up at the community center too, so I needed to get in and out before he arrived.

The meal delivery volunteers used the community center kitchen to store and prep their meals and one of the back offices for their business needs. I'd volunteered for the program during my summers home from college and knew Bonnie, the program manager anyway, so stopping by would be nice. She was in the kitchen prepping food when I arrived.

"Well, look what the cat drug in." She wrapped her arms around me in a big bear hug. "I've missed your sweet face, Lilybit. Why haven't you come to see me sooner? Your momma would be disappointed in you."

She was right. My mother would have been disappointed, but thankfully Colorado was too far away for them to hear the town gossip—at least I hoped it was. "I know, and I'm sorry, Miss Bonnie. You know my intentions are good, it's just that time gets away from me sometimes with my business being so busy and all."

She smiled and sat back down in the chair behind her desk. "I know, I know. Happens to all of us." She patted the cushion on the chair next to hers. "Come on over here and sit a spell. Tell me what you've been up to."

I did as she asked. "I'm good. Just working hard. I'm handling the sale of Myrtle Redbecker's property, and I wanted to ask about the person who delivers the food to her."

"Oh, that would be Grace Jeffers. Sweet as a peach, that girl is. You might not know her. She's a few years younger than you. Nineteen, I think. Lives on the outside of the county, off Jot Em Down Road. Mom's the one that runs the Dollar Plus store over there at the red light on Doc Majors Road and the highway. Never had a daddy that I know of."

I knew the store, but I didn't recognize the name. "I think I know," I lied. I definitely needed to go to church Sunday.

"Poor girl. Said she's heartbroken about Myrtle, too. Those two got on like two peas in a pod, but that's how she is with all our elderly. Why, I have to call her on that cellular phone of hers and make sure she isn't spending too much time with each of our customers 'cause the other ones get fussy if they don't get their meals on time."

"I remember that. They are very particular, aren't they?"

"They most certainly are, and rightfully so. Those meals mean a lot to them. Sometimes it's the healthiest thing they get all week, and they only get them once or twice, depending on how much they qualify for. I've been pushing to make it unlimited, but I've only got so much food to go around, what with relying on a limited budget and donations and all."

I reminded myself to write a check from the business and drop it by. "When is Grace supposed to deliver again? I'd like to talk to her."

"Oh, she's taken a temporary leave. Said she's just all torn up about what happened."

"I'm right there with her." We chatted a little longer about the program and how things were going, and I promised to come by more often. I meant it, I just wasn't sure I'd be able to as much as I'd like.

We said goodbye, and she squeezed me into another massive bear hug, nearly knocking the wind out of me. I rushed out to my car and headed toward the office, checking my rearview mirror for county sheriff cars behind me but there were none in sight.

* * *

I had a handful of voicemails from the three bidders on Myrtle's property waiting to be heard in my voicemail, and an inbox of emails at least six pages long. I often wondered how the big city realtors managed their time. Did they get everything done before they left for the day, or was their inbox a never-ending pit of email nightmares like mine? How did they have personal lives? My life had to be slower and easier, and I still felt rattled most of the time.

I promised Belle lunch for a week if she'd follow up with everything that didn't have to do with the Redbecker property and swore I'd never ask her to do anything like that again, but she called me a liar, and we both knew she was right. She gladly took on my extra work because that's what she did, and I knew she was invaluable and irreplaceable. She knew it too.

Each bidder had heard about Myrtle's death and wanted to know how to proceed. I directed each of them to her attorney, explaining the option to sell was still on the table through the trust with me still presiding as the selling agent, but that I had discovered a possible issue with the plot survey and wanted to follow up on and provide those details so each of them could make any changes to their bids if necessary. It was the best stall tactic I could come up with on the fly, and I thought it was a pretty good one.

I left the survey maps in my car but had a pretty good idea of the differences in the opinions of where the lines should be and wondered how I could find out the truth.

"What about the Georgia Historical Society?" Belle asked. She always answered my questions when she heard me talking to myself.

"That might be an option, but I'm not sure. The Pickett's and the Redbecker's have been in this town forever. They're well connected. Definitely more so than the Waddell's, that's for sure."

"Why do you say that?"

I rubbed my fingers and thumb together. "Money talks, and the Waddell's never had much of it." I spun around in my chair. She pulled up the Internet on her laptop and searched the Georgia Historical Society.

"Maybe they'll have records dating back to around the Civil War for this area."

"That's something to consider. Sonny did mention his family has owned the property since at least then."

"Hold on. I'm checking to see how far back their records go." She tapped into her laptop. "Says here some records go back as far as the 1600s in the Colonial states."

"And Georgia was a Colonial state."

"You get an A for your knowledge of state history."

"As if that wasn't drilled into our brains all through school."

"Good point."

I called the information number listed on the Georgia Historical Society's website and explained the situation to Clara, the woman who answered. She said they might have what I needed but she'd have to check. I gave her my contact information and made a note in my planner to follow up in two days. "Hopefully, this'll do the trick."

"So, what now?" Belle asked.

"I need a new squeegee for my shower."

"Okay."

My cell phone rang. I snuck a peek at the caller ID. It read Dylan. I hit decline. "I'm thinking I can probably get that at Dollar Plus."

"I saw that, you know."

"I'll call him later."

"You're going to have to deal with him eventually."

"He's just going to lecture me for not doing what he said."

"That's not what I'm talking about, and you know it."

I did know it, but I didn't want to deal with it with her, either. "I really need that squeegee."

"Don't think I don't know the real reason you stayed at my place last night."

"I'll pick up lunch."

"If your momma were here, she'd be on my side."

"Probably," I said, and let the door to our office slam behind me. "And thank God she's not," I said under my breath. I knew she was right about that. My mother loved Dylan probably more than she loved me, which was why I hadn't called her and told her any of what had happened.

* * *

I recognized the woman at the Dollar Plus cash register right away. I'd seen her around town and realized I knew her daughter, too. Grace Jeffers sat on the opposite register's counter, filing her nails with a stainless-steel nail file like my mother used. I hated those because I always worried I'd file too hard or the pointed tip would puncture my skin somehow.

Both Grace and her mother were regular attendees at my church, as was most of the town, but Grace also sang in the church choir. She'd been the lead solo girl for a few years, and every time she sang, most of the church thought she should try out for one of the singing shows on TV.

"Hi Grace," I said.

Her eyes stayed glued to her nails. "Hey."

I waved my hand in the space between her nails and her face. "Sorry to bug you, but I'd like to talk to you about Myrtle Redbecker."

That caught her attention. She dropped her hands to her lap and stared at me. "She's dead."

"Yes, I know. I'm her, or I was her real estate agent, and I—" I waved my hand in the air. A kid her age didn't care about the details. "Basically, I need to ask you a few questions that might help clear up some things regarding the sale of her property."

Her eyes shifted to her mother who had stepped over to listen. "It's all right honey," she said. "Go ahead." She stuck out her hand. "I'm her momma, Sheila Jeffers."

"Lily Sprayberry."

"Oh, sweetie, I know. I see your real estate signs all over town, and we go to church together. Nice to meet you."

"You, too."

"What kind of questions?" Grace asked. "All I did was bring her food. I didn't really know her all that well."

That's not exactly how Bonnie said it, I thought. "You deliver on Sunday, right?"

She nodded.

"I used to volunteer for Meals Made for You too, and when I delivered the food, I usually helped the customers get it ready. Sometimes I'd sit and talk with them for a bit."

"So?"

"Do you do that?"

"Not really. They get cranky if they don't get their food when they're supposed to."

"I can understand that. "So, how long did you spend with Mrs. Redbecker on Sunday?"

"I didn't see her Sunday."

"Did she not have a planned delivery?"

"She did, but when I went by, she didn't answer the door."

"About what time was that?"

She adjusted her legs on the counter. "I don't know, maybe sixish? I'm not really sure."

"Can you tell me what happened when you went there?"

She leaned over and grabbed a pack of bubble gum from the candy area of the counter and opened it. She unwrapped a piece of gum and chewed while she talked. "I went there, got the food out of my car and knocked on her door. When she didn't answer, I put the food back in my car and left."

"Did you hear anything inside her house?"

She shook her head. "Nope."

"Did you see anyone inside?"

"I wasn't exactly looking in the windows or anything."

"Of course not. How about outside? Did you notice anyone outside?"

"I saw that Mr. Luna dude walking back to his house. Said he was leaving something on Mrs. Redbecker's porch. Something he'd borrowed from her, but I didn't pay much attention."

"Did you see Sonny Waddell? He lives on the other side of Myrtle's."

She shook her head. "I know Mr. Waddell. Used to deliver to him, but he stopped ordering. Said the food sucked."

"Okay. You didn't happen to see any cars in her driveway or notice anything out of the ordinary, did you?"

She shrugged. "Wasn't really looking." She jumped off the counter. "I gotta go. I'm meeting some friends up at the lake."

I picked a packet of Tic Tacs from the candy section and tossed it on the counter along with a five-dollar bill, thanked Grace's mother and left.

I called Belle from my cell phone. "Sonny Waddell said Grace Jeffers saw him outside after he went to Myrtle's, but Grace said she didn't see him." I pulled onto the highway. "Why do you think he'd lie about that?"

"Why do you think he's the one that's lying?"

"What reason would Grace Jeffers have to lie?"

"Because she's a teenager, and a lot of them do it because they can."

"Don't be so negative, Belle. It's ugly."

"I'm not negative. I'm realistic."

"Either way, one of them is lying."

"Maybe it's time to give Dylan a call?"

"Ugh." I would have preferred to have a root canal than willingly engage with my ex-boyfriend, and I feared the dentist more than clowns. "I was thinking I'd wait until I had a notebook full of things to discuss with him. That way I could just go through the list and get it all done at once."

"You're so scared my daddy couldn't drive a watermelon seed up your behind with a sledge hammer."

I laughed. "Because he's always wanted to do that."

She laughed too. "That's still my favorite saying ever."

"Your dad has some great ones."

"And they're fitting at times, too." She coughed. "Like now. Don't be a wimp. Make the call. Now's as good a time as any." The line went dead.

She was probably right, but I didn't take orders from her, especially ones that required me to step out of my comfort zone and wear my heart on my sleeve. Sure, I could call the Sheriff's Office during an emergency, but this had baggage to it, or at least it felt that way, even though it was about the murder investigation, so I opted to drive back to Myrtle's property and check on it instead. I might have been stalling the inevitable, but I still had a job to do, and part of that job included keeping an eye on my client's property. I felt a stronger sense of urgency to uphold my responsibilities because of Myrtle's murder and an intense need to babysit her property more than I would a normal client.

* * *

The crime scene tape had been removed from the front door, and since the realtor key box was still on the door handle, I saw no reason why I couldn't run in and check on things. After all, it was my duty.

The handle turned easily in my hand, and I flinched. "Not again," I whispered. "Please don't let me find anyone dead. Please don't let me find anyone dead." I opened the door slowly and tiptoed inside, gently closing it door behind me.

I barely recognized the entire entryway area. Someone had attacked the walls and floors with an ax. I ran my fingers over the holes in the walls and crouched down to pick up the broken photos lying on the floor. Just then, something heavy crashed to the kitchen floor, the thunk sound it made when it hit echoed down the hall. I froze.

Whoever had destroyed Myrtle's house was still inside, and whatever they were doing, they no longer tried to hide. Banging and smashing sounds reverberated from the kitchen. I sprinted down the short hall and caught a glimpse of someone dressed in black sweats and a black hoodie running out the backdoor and across the back yard into the wooded area of Myrtle's property. I bent over to catch my breath, grabbing the edge of the kitchen counter to balance myself, and that's when I saw Junior Goodson lying on the floor on the other side of the kitchen counter, exactly where I'd found Myrtle the day before.

He twisted his neck to the side and held his hand to his forehead. "Man, that hurts. I think I need an ambulance."

I finally made that call to Dylan.

* * *

Dylan dragged me from Myrtle's front porch and the gathering crowd over to the back side of her house. "What do I have to do to make you understand you need to stay out of this investigation?"

"I wasn't trying to meddle in your investigation, Sheriff." I made my frustration obvious with the accent placed on the word sheriff. "I simply came by to check on my property listing. The door was unlocked, and it shouldn't have been, so given the circumstances, I thought I should check."

"What you should have done was call me immediately. You could have been killed."

I didn't exactly have an argument for that. "I'm sorry."

He took off his hat and rubbed his short hair. "Did you do this kind of stuff before I came back to town, or are you doing this because I'm the sheriff now?"

"Really?"

He paced up and down the side of the house. "From now on, just…just stop going into homes alone, okay?"

I folded my arms across my chest. "I'm a realtor, remember?"

He threw his hands up. "Well, maybe you should consider another career then."

"You did not just say that."

"I don't want you getting killed on my dime."

"Then I'll try very hard to get killed on someone else's dime. I promise."

He let out a frustrated sigh. "That's not what I mean, and you know that. I don't want anything happening to you."

"I wasn't trying to let anything happen to me. I was checking on my client's property." That wasn't a lie, and it wasn't an embellishment. I really was concerned. "Was it smart? Probably not, and yes, I probably should have called you, but I didn't think someone would be in there in the middle of the day like that."

"Anything can happen when money's involved. Remember that next time, okay?"

"I will."

He asked me to reiterate what happened, so I went over it again. Billy Ray Brownlee had fixed Junior right up with a Band-Aid and sweet tea, but Dylan kept him on Myrtle's couch for questioning. I stuck around to listen.

"If you were here to do lawn work, why'd you come inside?" Dylan asked.

He walked into the kitchen and pointed to the empty thermos on the counter. "It's hot out. I wanted to refill my water jug."

"About how long were you inside?"

"Two, maybe three minutes before I was attacked."

"Did you know anyone was in the house?"

"Not at first, but I heard some pounding noises upstairs. Figured it was Jesse, so I just ignored it. Got some ice, and the next thing I know, I'm on the ground, and Lily over there is calling you."

"You didn't see who hit you?"

"No, sir, but I'm guessing it was Jesse."

"What makes you think that?"

Junior stared at him. "Known him all my life. Know what he'll do, and how he'll do it."

"Did he say anything to you?"

"No, sir."

"Did you hear him come into the room?"

"No, sir, but I had the water on, and I was washing my hands, so I wasn't really paying attention. Like I said, I figured it was Jesse looking for the money is all, so I wasn't really concerned."

"But why not?" I asked.

Dylan raised his eyebrow at me.

"I saw Jesse tell Junior to stay off the property. He was pretty upset, too." I made eye contact with Junior. "I guess I'm wondering why you didn't take that seriously."

Junior laughed. "Jesse don't scare me. Besides, I made a promise to Mrs. Redbecker, and that trust is paying me to do a job, so I got to do it."

"What happened between you and Jesse? You two used to be so close?"

Junior rubbed the back of his head. "A lot of nothing, really. He just wasn't the same after his ma and pa died. Couldn't get himself right and that got between us. Got between a lot of stuff in his life I guess, so we kind of parted ways."

I peered out the kitchen window. Someone had dug holes throughout half the backyard. "Junior, is that your handy work out there?"

He shook his head. "Safe to say that's Jesse looking for the money."

"So, you know about the money, too?" Dylan asked.

"Most everyone knows about the money," Junior said.

"What are you doing on the property now?" I asked.

"Just finishing up on the River Birch tree work I told Mrs. Redbecker I'd do for her."

I scanned the backyard further.

"Tell me what you know about the money," Dylan said.

"Don't know much. Just that Old Boone Pickett stashed it somewhere on the property. Might even be in the house. Don't know for sure."

"But you believe there is money possibly buried somewhere on the property?"

"Yes, sir."

"Or you believe there's a chance it's hidden inside the house somewhere?"

"Yes, sir. Way I was told, Boone Pickett didn't say one way or another if it was inside or out, so Jesse's probably wanting to tear everything apart looking for it."

Dylan acknowledged him with a nod. "He ever ask you to help him find the money?"

"No, sir."

"He ever come out and say he wanted to try and find it himself?"

"No, sir. We never talked much about it, really."

"Why do you think he's looking for it now?"

"Guessing the bank's looking to foreclose on that garage of his if he don't catch up on the payments."

"You think he's behind on a business loan?" I asked.

"That's what I hear. Something about taking out a loan against the garage for a business deal gone bad. Don't know the details, but it sounds like something Jesse would do."

Dylan used his cell phone to take photos of the kitchen. "I think that's it for now, Junior. I'll let you know if I've got any more questions, but I think it's best you stay clear of the property until the investigation is over."

Junior shrugged. "If that's what I got to do, then I guess it's all right."

"It's what you've got to do," Dylan said.

"It's probably best," I said.

"You planning on arresting Jesse?" Junior asked.

"For what?"

"For attacking me."

"But you said you didn't see him come at you, so you can't be sure it was him."

Junior shook his head. "No, sir, but don't know who else would do it."

Dylan tilted his head at me. "Did you get a good look at the perpetrator?"

I shook my head. "Not really. All I saw was a big blur of black sweats running away."

"Can you guess height and weight maybe?"

I closed my eyes and tried to focus on the image but nothing came up. "I can't. I'm sorry. It's all just a big blur." How did people remember that kind of stuff in the heat of the moment?

"You can press charges Junior, but it'll be your word against his, and I'm not sure a judge won't drop them once he goes up for bail."

Junior dropped his chin to his chest and exhaled. "Aw man, it ain't worth it." He'd been sitting at the kitchen table and stood. "I just want to get home and have myself a beer."

We maneuvered our way to the front door and walked Junior outside. He asked if he could gather his stuff, and Dylan helped him load his pickup with his push mower, a few shovels and a couple of rakes. He climbed in the car and before he drove off, Dylan grabbed a shovel leaning against the window just inside Myrtle's front door. "You forgot one," he yelled to Junior.

Junior flipped around in his seat. "Oh, that ain't mine."

It was the same shovel propped up against the window on the day I discovered Myrtle dead.

CHAPTER FOUR

Belle and I sat at a table outside of Millie's enjoying our sweet tea and talking girl talk. "You are just destined to be in the middle of this thing, aren't you?"

"Apparently so, though not because I choose to be."

She twisted her phone toward me. "I think I'm getting this. Hit play."

I angled the phone so the sun wouldn't blind the screen from my view and hit the play button. A sweet little beige puppy yelped into the camera. "Oh, my goodness, it's adorable." The puppy bounced and barked—or at least attempted to bark but it sounded more like a cough—its floppy ears flapping as it spoke, until the video ended. "Are you really getting it?"

"For you. I'm getting it for you."

I handed her back her cell. "You are not."

"I'm not kidding. You're going to need something to keep you company throughout your old maid years."

"I'm twenty-six. I'm nowhere near the old maid years."

"They start at twenty-eight." She sipped her tea. "The dog is two months. He's a Boxer mix. I checked, and they live about twelve years, so he'll be around to get you through the worst part, but you'll have to find another dog for the rest of it. Or, maybe you can get a cat then. Whatever works."

"You're funny."

She stared at me with absolutely no expression on her face whatsoever.

"Stop that."

"Where's your phone?"

"Why?"

She held out her hand and wiggled her fingers at me, palm up. "Where's your phone? Give it to me."

"No."

"Come on." She wiggled her fingers again. "Give it to me."

"No," I said with more intensity.

"Fine. If you don't want to call Dylan and dump this garbage between the two of you, then I'm getting you the dog. I don't want my best friend being alone the rest of her life. I am far too pretty and smart to have an old maid for a best friend. That will ruin my rep."

I laughed. "Ah, now the truth comes out. This is all about you."

She giggled. "No, it's about you. And the puppy. I love that puppy." She hit play on the video again. "I mean seriously, look at that face. How adorable is that?"

"He really is adorable. Why don't you get him?"

"My landlord doesn't allow pets."

"I know an excellent realtor."

"Well, howdy you two. I was fixin' to call you today, Miss Lily." Odell Luna walked up behind Belle. I was grateful for his interrupting the puppy conversation. The last thing I needed was the responsibility of a puppy.

"Hello to you too, Mr. Luna," Belle said.

"Hi, Odell. What were you planning to call me about?"

"I've decided I'm going to go ahead and put my property up for sale. Figured I'd entertain those big builders who keep calling me about them condos. Thought I'd talk with you about signing a contract. I don't know much about that stuff but I trust you do."

Just then my cell phone rang. I checked the caller ID and showed it to Belle. "It's the Historical Society." I smiled at Odell. "Odell, I need to take this. Can you give me just one minute? Belle can give you a few quick details on how we can get started with the sales process."

"I sure can," Belle said.

I stepped away to answer my phone as Sonny Waddell marched up, his chest thrust out and arms swinging. His flared nostrils pushed air out so loudly I heard it above the ring of my phone. He headed straight for Odell Luna. I motioned for Belle to run for cover, but her eyes locked onto Sonny's approach and wouldn't detach.

The man was about to blow and I knew it would be ugly.

"What kind of crazy are you doing, Odell?" Sonny's voice boomed right into Odell's face.

I stepped back a bit and covered my phone's mic to drown out Sonny's yelling. "This is Lily Sprayberry."

"Ms. Sprayberry, this is Clara Smith from the Georgia Historical Society. I'm calling to let you know I should have something to you on that property by tomorrow morning. I'm sorry for the delay, but I've had to do a more detailed search than I expected."

I'd only half heard her, mesmerized by the verbal altercation happening between the two old men. "Oh, I…that's okay. I understand."

"Thank you. I'll either be calling you tomorrow, or I'll send you something via email."

"Okay, I appreciate it. Thank you so much for letting me know." We disconnected, and I stepped through the gathering crowd to separate the two men, bumping into Grace Jeffers in the process.

"Sonny, Odell." I wormed my way in between the two. "Enough. You're both acting like kindergarteners. Goodness, this is not proper behavior now, is it?"

Sonny's face remained blood red, and a vein running up the middle of his forehead throbbed. "He's trying to force me to sell my property by ganging up with you and that dead woman's trust, that's what he's doing. Thinks he can get more for his land if I sell mine along with y'all, but I ain't doing it." He poked his finger toward my chest. "And I'm getting what's rightfully mine no matter who ends up buying that old bat's property."

I flinched. "Sonny, nobody is trying to make you do anything—"

He interrupted me. His voice louder, his eyes, cold and hard, glaring at me. "Don't think I don't know what's going on here. This ain't no Hatfield and McCoy feud. The Waddell's ain't never going to make up with the Pickett's, I can dang gum guarantee that."

Selling the land to the builder might end the reason for the feud, but the bitterness attached to it wouldn't stop until the remaining Pickett's and Waddell's died, and since Jesse wasn't married, and Sonny's children had moved away years ago, that could happen sooner than Sonny realized.

Jesse Pickett had horrible timing—or perfect timing, depending on who you asked—bursting into the mix and shoving poor old Odell Luna aside at that very moment. "There ain't no feud to be making up about, old man. That property don't belong to your family and it never did."

"Oh, this is getting good," Belle said. She'd finally pushed herself up from the chair and moved over near the crowd.

I shook my head. "Belle."

She bit her lip. "Sorry."

Sonny's height didn't match the younger man's, but he outweighed him by at least an average sized Pit Bull. He balled his hands into fists and held them up near his chest. "Come on boy, how 'bout we settle this now?"

"Oh, dear Lord," I stepped in between the two. "Come on already, Sonny. Stop it. You're too old to be acting like this." I grabbed his bicep—which was pretty solid for a man his age—and did my best to direct him to the seat I'd been in earlier, but he wouldn't budge.

"Leave me alone," he yelled. He pulled his arm loose. "And don't you go and touch me. You're part of the reason this is happening. You young people think you can change things around here. Think you can make it all big and fancy like the city, but ain't nobody all that interested in that. Some of us like it the way it is. You want to sell them big city condominiums, then you go and move to Atlanta and sell them there and leave us alone." He shook his finger at me. "Make sure that property don't sell or else."

"That property belongs to me, and I'm not selling it, no matter what Lily here says," Jesse said.

"You know darn good and well part of that property belongs to the Waddell family, and if I have to put you in a grave next to your aunt to get it, then that's what I'll do."

The crowd responded with shocked oh's and ah's.

"And here we go," Belle said.

"Belle, please."

She held her hands up, palms facing me. "Sorry."

"Gentlemen, this is not the time or place for this discussion." I angled myself toward the growing crowd, my eyes making contact with Junior Goodson immediately. He offered me a slight nod.

Jesse laughed. "Well look at little Lilybit. Her boyfriend's the sheriff now, so she thinks she's got some authority here in town." His lips formed a thin, straight line and his eyebrows furrowed together, the number eleven forming between them.

I stood straight, doing my best to keep my voice steady as I spoke. "He's not my boyfriend."

He leaned his head toward me and laughed, a slow, soft laugh. "Right. You think you can tell us what to do now that your big boyfriend is back in town." He stepped into my personal space, forcing me to back up into one of Millie's tables. "Thing is Lilybit, I don't care who your boyfriend is. You don't got no authority over me."

"But I do."

The sound of Dylan's voice gave me the touch of confidence I needed. I smiled just as Jesse's cocky snarl warped into a worried frown. His shoulders sunk as he slowly pivoted toward Dylan.

"We're just having a discussion here, Sheriff."

Dylan squeezed my hand. "You okay?"

I nodded.

"Looks like this conversation is over," Dylan said.

Jesse pointed at Sonny. "You going to arrest him?"

"For what?"

"He threatened me."

Dylan sought my eyes for confirmation.

"Things got a little heated between the men. They might need some time to cool off."

Millie barged through her café door. "I called you to come get them all and throw them in the slammer for disturbing the peace." She wrapped an arm around me. "Except for sweet Lilybit here. She was just trying to keep them from killing each other."

Dylan glanced at Belle. "You agree with Millie?"

"About the men or Lily?" She laughed.

As did Dylan.

"I don't remember what was said exactly, but there's a lot of animosity between the three of them."

Dylan placed his hands on his side, dipped his head, shook it and sighed. When he raised it, his frustration was obvious. "All this training to handle a good old boy bar fight in the middle of town."

"Pretty much," Belle said.

"And a murder," I added.

"Come on boys," Dylan said, pointing to Odell, Sonny and Jesse. "You're coming with me."

* * *

After the crowd dispersed, Millie gave me and Belle free scones and fresh sweet teas. She chatted with us for a bit, trying, I assumed, to get some dirt on the debacle, but we stayed tight-lipped, offering just the occasional adjective and exclamation when necessary. Being in the center of the drama was bad enough but being a business in the center of the drama could destroy our business, and neither of us wanted that to happen.

Millie finally gave up, and Belle and I had an opportunity to speak freely.

She let her arms fall to her sides and sank down in her seat. "Wow. Small town life sure isn't what it used to be, is it?"

"Not a bit."

"I honestly thought there was going to be a beat down between Jesse and Sonny, and my money would have been on the old man."

I shifted in my seat. "I was thinking."

"About?"

"About the note at my house. I don't think Jesse left it."

"Okay. Who do you think did then?"

"Sonny Waddell."

"Because of today?"

I nodded. "Yes, but it's more than that. It's something he said."

She stared at me. "Well, what did he say."

"Oh, he said, make sure that property don't sell or else."

"Okay, well, he doesn't want the property to sell because he thinks part of it belongs to him. We both know that."

"That's not it."

"Then what is it?"

"That's exactly what the note at my house said."

"Oh, that's not good."

"I can't help but think maybe Jesse is innocent now."

"Maybe you're right. Are you going to talk to Dylan?"

"Yes, but first I'm going to talk to Jesse. After work. I've got a lot to catch up on."

She rolled her eyes. "Lord girl, work can wait. You should talk to Dylan. And didn't he tell you to stay away from all of this?"

"Would it matter? It seems to find me lately, don't you think?"

"You're right. I just wish you had the dog already. We'll have to have him trained to bite mean guys in their sensitive spot in case something like this happens again."

"I'm not getting a dog."

"I know you're not. I'm getting you the dog. For your birthday."

"It's not my—oh my gosh. My birthday is coming up, isn't it?"

"Yes, in three days."

I guzzled down the last of my sweet tea. "I can't believe I forgot. Is that a sign of old maid-dom? Maybe I am becoming one?"

Belle threw her hand up into the air. "That's what I said."

My jaw dropped. "I was kidding. Gosh. Way to make me feel old."

"What can I say? The clock is ticking Lily. I mean, seriously, even Junior Goodson is dating, and no one ever thought he'd find a girl. Did you see the little cutie he was hanging out with earlier?" She coughed to disguise her laugh, a tell-tale sign she was giving me a hard time.

"You mean Grace Jeffers from Meals Made for You? I wouldn't say they were hanging out. More like standing next to each other."

"Wait, that's the girl you told me about?"

I nodded.

"She sings at church. She's really good, and they were definitely hanging out."

"You think?"

"Absolutely. I even caught them doing a shoulder bump and laughing once, so there is definitely something going on there."

"Huh."

"She's pretty young, right?"

"Bonnie said around nineteen."

"Ew. That's practically a baby compared to Junior."

"I know. It's kind of gross." I tried to imagine what it would be like if I went out with a nineteen-year-old boy, but I couldn't. "Well, all I can say is if dating someone seven years younger than me is the only way I won't be an old maid, then that's just too bad. I'm actually not all that worried about being an old maid anyway. I'm happy doing my own thing, and I like having my independence. I'm not interested in trading it in, not for something like that at least."

Belle laughed. "You are not becoming an old maid. I was just kidding. I'm not kidding about the dog though. I really think you need a dog."

I would have preferred her joke about my being an old maid over the dog. I didn't have time for a dog, though that puppy was awful cute. "Let me see the video again." I shook my head. "No, wait. I do not need a dog."

She leaned toward me. "Someone, probably Sonny Waddell, a very angry old man, entered your home and left a threatening note, someone that very likely murdered your client, and that someone was also most likely in that same client's house two times while you were there." She straightened. I am absolutely getting you a dog, and we're training that dog to defend you."

There wasn't one point in any of that I could argue, so I didn't even try. "I'm heading to the office. You coming?"

"You don't want to go see the puppy?"

"Uh, no. Not right now anyway. I've got some calls to make. Maybe next year."

"Chicken."

"Absolutely."

* * *

The unusually high foot traffic outside our office window had to be because of everything going on, so I closed the blinds.

Belle laughed. "Bless their hearts. They can't help themselves."

"I swear, they're all slowing their gait and staring at me."

"You should run for the county fair queen this summer."

"Why on earth would I do that?"

"You're hugely popular right now." She skipped over to the window, pulled up the blind, and waved at the onlookers, who quickly walked away. "I'm pretty sure you're more popular than Sally Sue what's-her-face."

"Who?"

"You know, the girl whose number was painted on the gas station wall in high school?"

I threw my pencil at her. It hit her forehead and bounced off.

"Ouch."

"Well, you deserved that."

"Yes, I did, but it was totally worth it."

Dylan coughed. "Some things never change, do they?"

I brushed a long, flyaway golden strand back behind my left ear and licked my lips before turning around to face him. "Hey. What's up? Did you release the boys?"

Belle laughed. "Boys. That's an accurate description considering how they behaved."

"My thought, too," Dylan said. He sauntered over to my desk all slow and steady, the way he used to when he'd see me coming toward him from a distance. It was all kinds of sexy and sweet rolled up in six feet of adorable. I hated it.

"Did Jesse press charges?"

"He wanted to, but I questioned each of them and explained that they all could press charges if they wanted, and surprisingly, none of them wanted to."

Belle snorted.

The corner of Dylan's mouth twitched.

"This really is a big mess." I bent my leg and tucked my left foot under my right hamstring.

Dylan pulled one of our conference table chairs over to my desk, flipped it around and straddled it, his legs wrapped around the back of the chair. It was the way he used to sit in high school, too. "I arrested Jesse."

"But I thought nobody pressed charges?"

"For his aunt's murder."

"Oh." I untangled my legs and repositioned them the same way, only opposite.

"What's wrong?"

"Nothing." I picked at a piece of lint on my pants.

His relaxed posture disappeared, replaced with tight, stiff shoulders and a corded neck. "Are you really going to do this?"

"Tell him about the note already," Belle said.

Dylan's eyes shifted from Belle to me. "Did you get another note?"

I shook my head. "No, I didn't get another one, but earlier today, during that whole thing with the guys, Sonny Waddell said exactly what was written on the note."

He pulled his note pad from his pocket and flipped through the pages. "Make sure that property don't sell or else?"

I nodded. "Word for word. Don't you think that's kind of strange?"

"That's a pretty basic statement. Any of those men could have written that."

"Well then, doesn't that at least imply reasonable doubt?"

"She's got a point there, Sheriff," Belle said.

"The evidence points to Jesse," he said.

"But doesn't it point to Sonny Waddell, too?" I asked.

"In a lesser way, I suppose so."

"I don't think it's all that less. He admitted to being at Myrtle's the night she was killed. He has a stake in the property being sold, too. His family has a long-standing property dispute with the Pickett family, and he's been heated and aggressive toward me and others a few times about it all. You should have seen him earlier. He threatened both Jesse and me."

"So, you're saying you think Sonny Waddell killed Myrtle Redbecker?"

I nodded slowly and then ended up shaking my head. "I honestly don't know."

"That's why you sell real estate and I'm a Sheriff."

"You were supposed to be a football player," I mumbled under my breath.

Dylan didn't say anything, but the furrowed brow and down-turned mouth told me he'd heard what I said.

He grabbed hold of the top of the chair back and pushed himself up. "I've got the note. How about I take another look at it? Will that make you happy?"

"Can you maybe check writing samples? You know, send it out to a forensic writing analysist or something?"

"This is Bramblett County Georgia, Lilybit. How much money do you think we have?"

"You know I hate it when you call me that."

He positioned his hat snuggly onto his head and nodded toward me. "Yes, ma'am. I know." He smiled. "I'll be in touch."

He smiled at Belle. "Ms. Pyott, always a pleasure."

Belle returned his smile. "Sheriff Roberts."

As he walked toward the door, I rushed over and stopped him. "When is Jesse's bail hearing?"

He checked his watch. "Judge is trying to clear his schedule for his last call this afternoon."

"That doesn't even give him time to get an attorney."

He laughed. "Best he can get is a public defender, and he's not getting out before his trial anyway, so he's got time to work the case." He offered me one last smile and walked out.

I didn't smile back.

I dragged myself back to my desk and dropped into my chair. "Great."

"What?"

"Remember that song my mom used to make us listen to all the time when we were in high school?"

"Which one? She made us listen to a lot of songs."

"The one she said her mom used to make her listen to all the time when she was a kid."

"Should I repeat my last statement?"

"The one Vicki Lawrence sang that Reba McEntire redid. 'That's the Night that the Lights Went Out in Georgia'."

"Oh, yeah. I always kind of liked that song. What about it?"

"I'm worried that's how Jesse will end up."

She sang the chorus, her voice chipper until the words made sense. "Oh. Yikes."

"Exactly."

"Do you think he's innocent?"

"I don't think so, but I'm going to find out for sure."

Chapter Five

The Bramblett County Jail hadn't had an upgrade in at least fifty years. As if the dismal gray cell walls weren't bad enough, years of allowing transient prisoners to smoke in them turned them a stained yellowish color, and the scent of old, stale cigarette smoke hung in the air like dead skunk on the road.

Most county jails don't let visitors go back to the cells, but Bramblett County was special. Actually, Dylan let me go back to the cell only because the visiting room was being cleaned since the most recent prisoner to be visited decided to defecate on the floor to show his angst over his imprisonment. I was promised once it was clean, Jesse and I would be moved to the room, and the smell would be reasonably better. Not fresh and flowery, but better.

Anything would be better than dead, smoky cigarette smell.

Jesse was surprised to see me and from the look on his face, maybe even a bit happy. "What're you doing here?"

"If I didn't know better, I'd say that you might just be happy to see me, Jesse Pickett."

His shoulders sank. "I'm sorry for being nasty to you, Lily." He held onto the bars of his cell. "I shouldn't be that way. My momma taught me better than that."

"I know for a fact she did, but it's okay. I forgive you."

"Why are you here?"

"I figured this would be the best place to have your full attention."

He laughed. "Guess you figured right. Not much else going on here."

Dylan came in and led us to the visiting room. We were the only ones there.

"Even less going on here," I said.

He nodded. "You want to know if I killed my aunt, don't you?"

"For starters I want to know if it was you that attacked Junior Goodson."

He rubbed the back of his neck, and that was all I needed to know he'd done it.

"Why'd you do it? And why were you in the house?"

"You know why."

"Are you trying to find the money? Did you kill your aunt?"

"Do you think I did?"

"The evidence is pretty damaging."

He hung his head. "They're going to lock me up for good."

"Not if you didn't do it."

He stared at me.

"Well?"

It don't matter none what I say now does it? They've already hung me out to dry."

"The judge is going to hear your case today for bail. Have you seen your public defender yet?"

He shook his head. "That don't matter either. Your boyfriend even said they ain't gonna let me out of here. Don't know why. I don't have a dime to my name. Can't go anywhere anyway." His voice was monotone, lacking emotion entirely.

I almost felt sorry for him, but I just couldn't decide what I thought. Half of my head thought he did it while the other half swore he was innocent. "I wanted to let you know I've contacted the Georgia Historical Society. If there are any records of the original property lines for the Pickett and Waddell properties, they'll let me know. That might at least clear up part of this whole mess."

"That man ain't getting any of my family property. It belongs to me."

I leaned toward his glassed-in room. "That's the thing Jesse, it doesn't. It belonged to Myrtle, and she left it to the trust, to be sold upon her death."

He smacked the glass with the palm of his hand. "That property is mine. I don't care if there's money buried on it or hidden in that house or not. She can't leave it to no trust. I'm her next of kin."

A deputy pushed through the door. "All right Mr. Pickett. Time to go." He gave me a slight smile. "Sheriff's in his office if you'd like to talk to him, ma'am."

"Thank you, but I've got to run." I headed out to my car more confused than before I visited Jesse.

* * *

The tiny courtroom had to be closed fifteen minutes before Jesse's bail hearing because most of the town showed up to watch, and the room only held twenty-four people.

The fire department came through and insisted everyone leave, but instead of going home, they ordered pizza and liters of Coke and stood outside waiting for the news.

Those twenty-four people left crowded in, and I didn't know who, but one of them forgot to hit the shower that morning. Part of me wanted to climb up on a chair and suggest everyone smell their arm pits, but I knew that wouldn't go over well.

I breathed a sigh of relief that Bramblett County hadn't become a country music song, and Jesse Pickett was given bail, but I doubted he'd be able to come up with the ten thousand dollars necessary to be released before his trial, which had yet to be set. His charge, first degree murder, was awfully harsh, but so was a blow to the head with a cast iron skillet, so I really couldn't object. Had Junior Goodson pushed to press charges for his attack, Jesse may had been spent a lot more time in the clinker.

The crowd had mixed feelings on his bail. Belle and I scoped everyone out, snooping without intention—okay, so we snooped with intention—hoping to determine what a trial with a jury of Jesse's peers might look like, and if things went the way it sounded, he'd spend the rest of his life behind bars.

"Look, see that?" She pointed to the backs of two people walking away from the crowd and down the main street through town. "It's them again. And they are definitely together."

I flipped up my sunglasses to get a better view. It was past five o'clock and the sun had already begun to dip down in the sky. "Is that Junior and Grace?"

"Yup. Told you so."

"That's just gross. She's too young for him."

"I don't know, maybe not. Men mature slower than girls."

"Still gross," I said.

"You just don't like Junior."

"I never said that."

"You don't have to say it, I can tell."

She was right, but I didn't think it was that obvious. "How?"

"Seriously? I'm your best friend. As if I don't notice the slight raise of the right side of your upper lip every time you see him or someone mentions his name? And I definitely notice the way you push back your face—which isn't the most flattering of looks if you must know the truth—every time you have to talk to him. I know all your little tics and tells. I have since we were what, ten?"

"I can't decide if I love you more for that or if it scares me."

"I suggest both."

"I think you're right."

She hooked her arm through mine. "Come on, I'll walk you to your car."

We walked past our favorite antique store that Santa always showed up and visited with kids at every holiday season, and the county library, which only opened the previous year, and I still hadn't picked up my card. "I need to get my library card."

"You better. Ellie Jean Pruitt is the librarian there now, and you know how tough she can be."

"Mrs. Pruitt? The librarian from high school?"

"That's the one."

"She wasn't tough. She loved me."

"Then you're the only person she loved."

"I doubt that, but if it's possibly true, I'd better get in there and get my card to maintain my good reputation."

Belle laughed.

* * *

I had several potential client leads to follow up on, a decluttering class I'd scheduled, promoted and filled with participants already booked for next month I'd yet to outline and create materials for, and a computer and planner full of regular work to get to, but instead, I decided to relax in a lavender salt bath with candles, soft music and a tall glass of sparking grape juice. Even though I didn't drink, I liked to enjoy something bubbly while I relaxed, so I always had my sparking grape juice in a champagne glass.

I closed my eyes and let the smooth, instrumental music and the warm water relax me and then that sweet puppy popped into my head. My eyes burst open. "Get out."

It popped in again. "No, really. Get out."

I watched the video replay itself over and over in my mind's eye. "I don't have time for a dog."

I talked as if someone was actually listening, as if they would talk back.

"I don't. I have a fulltime job. No, not a job. A career. I'm a business owner. I'm out late sometimes. How can I get home to let a dog out? What if it starves? Or poops on my floor?"

I glanced at my phone propped in the speaker unit on my bathroom counter. "Okay, so it's not even seven o'clock but that doesn't mean this happens every night." I held my nose and dunked myself under the water. I figured it I drowned myself I wouldn't have to worry about the puppy because I'd be dead.

Only that didn't work because apparently my body had some innate will to breathe and forced my head out of the water where the puppy thoughts lived. "I do not have time for a puppy."

A text came through, getting me out of my argumentative state and shutting down my music temporarily. Unfortunately, it killed my relaxed mood and when I couldn't get it back, I stepped out of the bath, dried off, dressed, and checked the message. It was from Dylan.

"Thought you should know Jesse's bail was paid. He's being released in the morning." He sent one more text that said, "Please keep an eye on your surroundings, and call me if you need me."

Jesse made bail? How was that even possible? Based on everything I'd heard, he was at risk of losing his garage because he couldn't pay his loans, so how could he come up with ten thousand dollars to get out of jail? If he owed money on his garage, I didn't think he could use it as collateral, but I wasn't sure. They never really covered that kind of thing in the TV shows. I wondered who would have paid it for him. Jesse never was the most popular guy in town, and though losing his family elicited empathy from some, being suspected of murdering his aunt seemed to negate that entirely. I wanted to know, but it was getting late, I was tired, and I didn't think I could handle an extended text or verbal conversation with Dylan at the moment, so I responded with a simple thank you and decided to find out later.

For the most part, I could talk with Dylan, but there were times when my emotions got the best of me, and talking—or even texting—to him drained me, and I just couldn't do it. I needed my space. Even though it had been years, his return to town opened up a barely healed wound that even sweet old Billy Ray Brownlee's Band-Aid couldn't make feel better.

I did find some comfort in knowing that guilty or not, Jesse Pickett hadn't become a Vicki Lawrence—Reba McEntire song. At least not yet.

I spent the rest of the evening avoiding my cell phone so I wouldn't watch the video of my cute puppy or have the urge to talk with Dylan. Instead I watched old episodes of *Monk* and *CSI* hoping they'd help me figure out who killed Myrtle Redbecker. I even Googled the question, but nothing came up.

And I thought Google had an answer for everything. Maybe everything that happened in metropolitan areas, but things that happened in Bramblett County didn't make it to the Internet.

Before finally closing my eyes for the night, I watched the video of my puppy one more time, giggling as he bounced and hopped and his adorable paws pushed on his cage. How someone could just abandon a sweet little guy like that puzzled me. His happy but sad face and floppy ears had me digging my heels into my mattress to stop myself from running out to get him right then. Not that the shelter was open at ten o'clock at night anyway.

Thank goodness, because I definitely didn't have the time for a dog. Definitely.

I checked my email one last time and saw that Clara Smith from the Georgia Historical Society had sent me a file. I opened the email and gave it a quick once over.

"Ms. Sprayberry, we have maps dating back to the 1500s but with respect to colonization and property rights, the best ones to determine legal rights for your area date back to about 1751. I'm attaching a scanned photo of the longitude and latitude coordinates for the specific area you mentioned along with the specific land rights information we have on file. Should you have any questions, please feel free to contact me, and I'll do my best to help again. Thank you."

I right clicked on the attachment and saved the image to my downloads, but not before opening it first to see who owned the section of land the two families had fought over for years. I wasn't sure if the answer was the one I expected, but I knew at least one person wouldn't be happy.

* * *

Millie's had a line out the door and past the antique store next door. "What's going on?" I asked the woman in front of me.

"Haven't you heard? She's got a new scone, and she's giving them away to random customers all day today."

Way to go with the effective marketing, Millie. Give something away, but don't tell them when. I loved that idea. "Do you know the flavor?"

"Sweet lavender."

My mouth immediately watered and all kinds of yummy thoughts kidnapped my brain. "That sounds delicious. I'm going to have to try it."

"Said everyone else in Bramblett County," Belle said from behind my right shoulder. "Millie knows how to work the scone business, that's for sure."

I almost knocked down the woman in front of me. "When did you get here? And seriously, don't sneak up on me like that." I leaned toward her ear and whispered, "I could have broken that poor woman's leg or something."

She laughed. "Either this murder has you all stressed out or it's Dylan being back in town, but whichever it is, you need a massage or something." She smirked. "Or something."

I elbowed her in the side. "Stop that." I knew my face was red by the heat penetrating from it. "And it's not because of Dylan. Someone paid Jesse's bail. He's being released this morning."

Her eyes widened. "Seriously? Who's stupid enough to do that?"

The woman in front of me leaned back and whispered, "If you ask me, I'd say Old Man Goodson, that's who."

I elbowed Belle again for not knowing how to whisper.

She bent to the side and rubbed it. "Ouch."

The woman turned around. "Guess he feels bad, what with his son causing all that trouble for Jesse back when his family died and all."

"What trouble?" Belle asked.

"You live under a rock or something?"

"No, ma'am. A sorority house in Athens, actually." The snootiness in Belle's tone wasn't discreet at all.

"Well, far as I'm concerned, it's the same thing."

"What happened?" I asked. My tone lacked the conceit of Belle's in an effort to maintain my good reputation and get an answer to my question.

"Oh, bless his heart, Jesse Pickett has had a time of it, and I don't think I should be spreading any more gossip about that poor boy."

"Of course. I understand. I'm working with the trust on his aunt's property, and I was just wondering if it has anything to do with why he and his aunt had a falling out." It was an honest question, and I was genuinely curious.

"I can't say one way or another, but Myrtle Redbecker was a nasty old woman who would have shot her own dog if it peed on her shoe, so I don't think it was anything that young man said or did."

The line moved closer to Millie's entrance, and she came out carrying a tray of scones just in time to save Belle from laying into the woman. "I've got me twenty-five of my new sweet lavender scones for the taking. Here's how it's going to work."

She detailed the directions, asking everyone to draw a number from the bowl her employee next to her carried. Millie then picked a number herself and everyone with that number got a free scone.

Everyone that didn't get a free scone dropped from the line and left, including the woman Belle nearly verbally accosted.

Cheapskates. Belle got a free one, but I didn't. She shared hers with me, and I stuck around and ordered us lattes and got myself a blueberry scone, too.

"Do you think he paid the bail?" Belle asked.

"Old Man Goodson?"

She nodded.

"I don't know, but I'm going to ask Dylan. He'll know." I tapped out a text.

She placed her elbows on the table and set her head in her hands. She flashed a big, toothy smile straight at me.

"What?"

"Nothing."

I kept typing. She kept toothy-grinning at me.

"What?"

"Look at you, all smiley and stuff while you text him."

"You're the one that's all smiley, not me."

"Uh huh."

"This is professional anyway."

"You're a real estate agent, how is this professional?"

"You know what I mean." I placed down the phone. "And just so you know, I thought about it, and I'm not getting my puppy. I just don't have time for him."

"Did you just hear what you said?"

"Yes, that I'm not getting the puppy."

"No, you said you're not getting my puppy."

"I did not."

"Yes, you did." She broke off a piece of my scone and ate it. "You are absolutely getting that puppy."

I had a feeling she was absolutely right, but I wasn't ready to admit that to her or even to myself.

My cell phone dinged. Dylan's text said, "Where are you?"

"Millie's."

"Be there in ten."

I set my phone down. "Great. Just great."

"What?"

"He's coming here."

She giggled. "Not only are you getting a puppy, you're getting back together with your ex." She leaned back and crossed her legs to the side. "It's almost like you're starting your own little family. What's your favorite flower?" She laughed. "Wait, it's a lily, right?"

"I need a new best friend. Savannah Emmerson is coming back to town to get her parent's house ready to go on the market. Maybe she and I can reconnect."

"Yeah, I can see that. You and the biggest—"

"Don't be rude."

"Well, you know she didn't act all that ladylike in college."

"Most girls didn't."

"Most girls didn't do things with their best friend's boyfriends."

"That's true, but she never did anything with Dylan."

"Probably not for lack of effort on her part."

"Lovely."

"Just a testament to the fact that you and Dylan are meant to be."

"Meant to be what?" Dylan asked.

I dropped my chin to my chest. The man had the worst timing ever.

"We were just discussing Savannah Emmerson. You remember her, don't you? She's coming back to town."

"Really? Bet there's a sellout of dead bolts at the hardware store."

I couldn't help myself. I laughed. So did Belle.

Dylan flipped around the chair next to me and straddled it. "Heard Millie's got a new scone. Either of you give it a try?"

Belle nodded. "Got me a free one. Lavender. It's fantastic, of course."

"Lavender is edible? I thought it was a bath soap or something."

I rolled my eyes. "Yes, and yes. Well?"

"Well, what?"

"Are you going to tell me who paid for Jesses' bail?

"Since it's public record, yes, I can tell you."

I waited.

He stared at me.

I waited some more, and when he didn't say anything, I huffed.

He smiled. "Old Man Goodson paid it."

"Oh my gosh, that nasty woman was right," Belle said.

"What nasty woman?"

I waved my hand. "Nothing. Why do you think he'd do that?"

"I had a similar question for him."

"What did he say?" Belle asked.

"Said he felt sorry for Jesse. Said the bad blood between the two boys always bothered him, and he felt he deserved something good in his life for a change."

"Wow. Just, wow," Belle said.

"Ditto," I said. I ate the last of my scone so Belle didn't get a hold of it. A few crumbs fell from my mouth as I spoke. "Did he say what exactly happened between the two?"

"No."

"Did you ask?"

"No."

"Why not?"

"It didn't seem relevant to the investigation."

"But Jesse told me to keep Junior away from the property, and Junior knows about the money possibly being buried there."

"Everyone in town knows there might be money buried on that land or hidden somewhere in that house, Lilybit. You want me to question the entire town?"

"Don't call me that, and now that you mention it, maybe?"

He pushed the chair forward and stood. "We have our suspect. The DA is building the case against him, and we'll go to trial. Jesse is going to be convicted, but in the meantime, I need you to stay clear of him, okay? I don't want anything to happen to you. Do you understand?"

I went to speak, but Belle interrupted me. "She understands, and don't worry. She'll be safe. She's getting a puppy."

His eyes shifted between us and finally landed on me. "A puppy? You?"

"I am not getting a puppy."

"A Boxer mix. He's adorable." She pulled her phone from her purse. "Want to see a video?" She tapped the screen on her phone and shoved it up into Dylan's face.

Tiny puppy sounds filled my ears, and my heart ached. Stay strong, I told my heart. You are not getting a puppy. You don't have time for a puppy. I had a feeling my heart thought differently, but I ignored the feeling.

"It's cute," Dylan said. "But a lot of work. You sure you have time for it?"

"I am not getting a puppy."

"She keeps saying that, but she is," Belle said. "You two can take it for long, romantic walks together."

I kicked her under the table.

"Ouch."

Dylan laughed and tipped his hat, said, "Ladies," and walked away.

I spit daggers at her. Theoretically speaking, of course. "I cannot believe you said that."

She chuckled. "What? That you're getting a puppy? You are, and you know it."

I gathered my things and walked away without saying another word.

* * *

I found myself on the outskirts of the county at Old Man Goodson's small engine repair shop. I hadn't consciously intended to go there, so when I arrived, I was a bit surprised. Old Man Goodson wasn't surprised to see me though.

"Wondered when you'd show up," he said as I entered the shop.

"Really? Why is that?" I admired the old antique tin signs hung throughout his shop. The Coke® ones were my favorite, but I got a kick out of the ones with the pin-up girls sitting on cars, too.

He handed me a bottle of cold water. "Here. Sit a spell. I'll tell you the story."

"I feel like you were expecting me or something."

"That woman your partner got sassy with this morning? She come by and told me you were asking questions. I figured you'd be stopping by, too."

Word got around fast in a small town.

I unscrewed the bottle of water and took a sip. I wasn't thirsty, just polite. "Do you think Jesse killed Myrtle?"

Something metal crashed in the back of the shop and landed on the ground. I jumped. Old Man Goodson took his time turning around and headed toward the sound. He tossed a few pieces of equipment I couldn't recognize around on the floor and then grabbed a broom resting against the wall.

"Darn rats. Can't seem to get rid of the little boogers."

I wanted to run out and vomit. I'd never been a fan of rats.

He wandered back my direction after scooting the varmint out the back of the shop. "Now, what'd you ask again?"

"I wanted to know if you thought Jesse killed his aunt."

"Oh, right. Sorry about that. Don't really know but figured the boy could use someone on his side for a change." He finished off his bottle of water and wiped the beads of sweat pooling on his brow. "Figured it ought to be me since I'm part of the reason he and Junior ain't friends no more."

"How do you mean?"

"If I'd kept my big trap shut, those two boys wouldn't have had their falling out and they'd still be friends. But because of me, Junior told Jesse his daddy might have had a fling with another woman that resulted in the making of another baby. A little sister for Jesse. One he never knew about."

Part of me felt empathy toward the guy, while another part of me saw even more reason for his desperation and angst.

"Do you think it's true?"

"Which part?"

"All of it."

He shrugged. "Lot of men have affairs. Wouldn't surprise me none if he did. Can't say if the kid is his or not, but that wouldn't surprise me none either."

I watched a bug crawl along a crack in the cement floor.

"I know what you're thinking," he said. He opened a can of tobacco chew and stuffed a pinch behind his bottom lip.

"You do?"

"You want to know who the kid is."

Actually, I wondered more about the mother, but the daughter interested me, too. "It's not my business." But yes, please tell me. Please. I hoped he heard my internal begging.

"Don't matter, I don't know who neither of them are anyway. Jesse's dad never said no names, and I never knew if he was telling me the truth either. We were drunk when he said it, and the next time it came up was when I asked, and he just laughed and said that was drunk man's talk was all."

"So how did Junior find out?"

"Overheard me fighting with the missus one night. She was giving me a what for, telling me how I wasn't good for nothing, and I said at least I didn't cheat on her and make no babies with another woman like Jesse's daddy did. Guess Junior heard that." He walked over the garbage can in the corner of the room and spit the chew into it. "Week or so later Junior and him got in an argument and the next thing I know they ain't friends no more. Happened shortly after his parents got killed. Poor timing on my kid's part, too." He stuffed more tobacco into his mouth. "Felt sorry for the boy."

"Do you know what happened with his aunt? Why they don't talk anymore?"

"Nothing like that if that's what you mean. At least not that I know of. Myrtle was always madder than a wet hen about something. When the boy lost his family, he come to her for help, and she shut him out. Slammed the door right in his face. Told him the bank of Redbecker don't help those that don't help themselves and wrote him right out of the family will. Didn't take much to make an enemy out of that old woman, that's for sure."

"Do you think there's really money on that property?"

He shook his head. "I think good ol' Boone Pickett is rolling over in his grave having a good old laugh right now. Way I heard it, the man was as cheap as the day is long. If he hid money, he hid it so good ain't nobody gonna be able to find it."

"So, what happens if you don't get your bond money back?"

"I won't get it back, but I knew that when I paid it."

"Why don't you get it back?"

"I couldn't afford to pay the whole amount, so I had to get one of those bail bondsmen to get a surety bond. They paid that, and I paid them a fee for it. Jesse had to promise to appear in court. If he don't then I got to come up with the rest of his bail and pay the bondsmen."

"Jesse will be there."

"I know." He tilted his head toward me. "You think he killed his aunt, don't you?"

"I wanted to think otherwise, but I can't get there."

He slowly nodded. "Kind of feeling that way, too. Shame. Watching a boy's life take that kind of turn."

I stood. "Yes, it is." I threw my empty water bottle in the trash. I didn't even realize I'd finished it off. "Thank you for filling me in on everything."

"Anytime, Lilybit. It's always a pleasure to chat with one of our home grown. You ever need your lawnmower or something fixed, come on down. I'll give you a discount."

"Thank you, Mr. Goodson."

* * *

I headed over to the office supply store in the next town over to print out the email and scanned maps from the Georgia Historical Society. I wanted six copies; one for myself, one for the attorney, the winning property bidder, Sonny Waddell, the county assessor's office and one to file with the state, if necessary. I needed them printed there so they could be notarized by the person that printed them. I wanted to make sure they were shown as direct from the Georgia Historical Society in the event that anyone tried to dispute their accuracy. Based on their information, over forty acres of land actually belonged to Sonny Waddell, not Myrtle Redbecker, and that changed not only the value of the land, but the plot lines, tax records, possibly even previous tax bills and a host of other things I wasn't even aware of.

Even though the sale of the property was already on hold, the information would just postpone it further. I all but kissed that forty-two thousand dollar commission–less business expenses, taxes and of course the split with my partner that I wasn't talking to at that moment—goodbye.

It never was the big clients that kept my business running. It was the little ones, and luckily, I had enough of those to keep my retirement fund growing.

The copies would take over an hour because of the six people waiting ahead of me, so I killed time and found myself at the animal shelter where the dog I had no intention of adopting resided.

The howling and barking immediately tugged at my heartstrings the moment I opened the shelter doors.

"I'm here to see the beige Boxer mix."

"Can you repeat that?" The woman behind the glass window asked. "It's hard to hear over the whining."

I got that. It was loud. "The beige Boxer mix. I'd like to see him."

"You mean Sparky? He was adopted this morning."

My heart fell to the ground and shattered into pieces. "But I just saw his video."

"We don't always have the chance to take them down right away. Listen, we're short staffed. It happens. Cut us some slack, okay?"

"I can't believe it."

"You wanna see another dog?"

"I was hoping to see him."

She slid the window shut.

I picked up the pieces of my broken heart and walked out. In my car I replayed the videos of the cute beige puppy that would never be mine, the one I said I didn't have time for, but suddenly wanted more than anything, and I sobbed.

I hoped whoever adopted little Sparky would love him as much as I'd realized I already did, and I hoped he loved them back as much as I wanted him to love me. Okay, maybe not that much, but close.

I gathered my composure, realizing his adoption was a sign and a good thing. I was not meant to have a puppy. My life wasn't right for a dog. If only I'd get a sign about Dylan, too.

* * *

I asked Dylan to meet me at Sonny Waddell's house. I explained what I'd learned from the Georgia Historical Society and said I wanted to give Sonny the good news, but I didn't feel comfortable going over there alone. He may not have been the one that killed Myrtle Redbecker, but he still got aggressive and threatening, and I had no intention of putting myself in harm's way.

As I pulled past Odell Luna's house, I noticed Jesse's car on the side of the road between Odell's and Myrtle's. I slowed to see if Jesse was outside, and saw Sonny storming out of Myrtle's front door with a shovel in his hand, the door slamming behind him. Hoping Sonny hadn't noticed me, I pulled to a stop and watched him lean the shovel against Myrtle's window and hurry back to his house.

How did he get inside? Was Jesse in there? If so, how did he get inside? If the house was damaged again, I'd pitch a fit the size of Texas. I called Dylan. "Hey, Jesse's at Myrtle's, and Sonny just came charging out of there. I don't feel good about this."

"Stay put. I'm on my way."

"I think I should check on the house. Jesse's probably in there destroying it."

"Lily, do not go inside. You hear me?"

I exhaled. "Yes, sir."

"Promise me."

"I promise. Geez." I pulled into Myrtle's long driveway and shut off my engine. I didn't want to break my promise, so instead, I go out of the car and snuck around back to peek inside the kitchen. I just wanted to see if I could see if Jesse had added any additional home demolition to the place.

Only from the looks of him, Jesse Pickett's days of home destruction were over. He lay on the kitchen floor with the back of his head smashed in just like his aunt had a few days before.

Chapter Six

After the coroner took Jesse's body, and a deputy arrested Sonny, I waited near my car for Dylan to tell me I could leave. He came out and handed me a bottled water. "Is this your thing now?"

"What do you mean?" I held my hands together to keep Dylan from noticing how much they shook.

"Finding dead bodies. Is it your thing?"

I swallowed hard. "I, uh…I don't think so. I mean, I sell real estate. I don't intentionally find dead bodies."

He removed his hat and leaned back against my car next to me. "That was a bad attempt at a joke. I apologize." He nudged his shoulder into mine, and I fought hard not to lean my head into him when I so desperately wanted to.

"It's okay."

"Sometimes in my line of work it makes it easier to crack jokes."

"Realtor jokes are a little less inappropriate."

"Tell me one."

"No. They're horrible."

"No, really. Tell me one."

"They're really bad, trust me."

"Come on. Just one. I promise I'll laugh."

"You always laughed at my jokes."

He turned toward me and smiled. "And I always will, Little Bean."

Don't cry, Lily. Do not cry. "Okay. A realtor has two property listings. Now add ten more. What does the realtor have?"

"Twelve listings?"

"No. Happiness. The realtor now has happiness."

He gave me a blank stare and then finally laughed.

I laughed, too. "I told you, they're horrible."

"Yeah, you were right."

"So, what happens now?" I asked.

"Sonny claims he didn't kill Jesse. Said he saw his car here, came by to tell him to leave, and found him dead. Was leaving to call us when you saw him."

"What about the shovel? He had it with him when he left."

"He claims it was lying next to Jesse, and he really doesn't have an explanation for taking it, but when he realized he did, he left it propped up against the front of the house where you saw him put it."

"I really don't think things can get any worse."

"I'm just glad you didn't get here sooner. I don't know what I'd have done if you'd have been killed, too." He dropped his head back and it would have rested on the top of my car if he wasn't so tall.

I found myself wanting to comfort him. "You're not getting rid of me that easily." Though you pretty much did a few years ago, I thought.

"I learned that a long time ago. No matter what I did, I couldn't get you out of my mind."

What? "Funny, that whole falling off the face of the earth thing you did said otherwise."

"I know, and I'm sorry about that." His shoulder touched mine.

I pushed myself off my car. "I'm not doing this. Not now. Probably not ever." I scurried around to the other side, hit the unlock button on my electronic key and climbed into the driver's seat.

"Lily, wait. Let me explain."

"Explain? Seriously? You had years to explain, but the statute of limitations on that has expired now." I shut the door.

"Come on, Lily. I came back here because of you, because of us."

"See, that's the thing Dylan. There isn't any us. You ruined that years ago." I started the ignition, kicked my car into reverse and left.

* * *

The office smelled like a floral shop exploded inside it and then someone cleaned up the explosion with lemon cleaner. When Belle needed to distract herself, she cleaned. A lot. The smells from the cleaning products and the dozen or so air fresheners she plugged into the unused outlets fought each other to take over my nose. My eyes watered within seconds of entering. I left the door opened to air out the fresh scent.

"Close that thing. You're letting all the good air out."

"If I don't let the good air out, my lungs will shrivel up and die. How many of those air fresheners did you plug in this time?"

She shrugged. "Under ten."

"I doubt that." I searched the electrical outlets and pulled out five hoping that would provide some relief. "What's got your gander up?"

Belle spun her office chair in a circle. "I don't know what's worse, the fact that Jesse Pickett is dead or that you just possibly ruined your chance at reuniting with the only man you've ever loved."

Oh boy. She went on a cleaning rampage because of me? Nope. I wasn't going to take the blame for that. Besides, I'd just found my second dead body of the week, and frankly, I was exhausted. "Thanks for making me feel better. I appreciate it."

She threw her hands up into the air. "Well, come on already. When are you going to cut that poor guy some slack?"

"First of all, I just found Jesse Pickett dead. We shouldn't even be having this discussion. Seriously. We should be respectful of the dead right now."

"You're right." She stuck out her bottom lip. "I am sorry. God rest his soul. May he find peace in heaven." She bowed her head. "And forgiveness if he did kill his aunt even though she was kind of a cranky old bat."

I didn't want to laugh, but it was hard not to.

"Is that better?" She smiled. "Now, can we get back to what you did?"

I pointed my right forefinger at her. "Oh, no uyou don't. Remember Jimmy what's-his-face from seventh grade?"

She tilted her chin up, and her nostrils flared. "You just wait a minute, missy. Don't you say his name out loud."

I raised my eyebrows and smirked. "Em hmm. That's who I'm talking about."

She straightened in her seat. "That's entirely different."

I laughed. "Exactly. You were in seventh grade and you still can't stand him for breaking your heart. I was nineteen, and Dylan and I dated for most of high school and part of college, and you think I should just forgive him and take him back. It absolutely is entirely different, just not the way you think it is."

"The boy whose name we shall not mention was my first love. Those are intense."

"As if I have no experience with that feeling."

She let out a long sigh and mumbled. "Fine, I'll forgive the boy whose name shall not be mentioned if you'll forgive Dylan."

"Jimmy moved away in eighth grade. There's no way to forgive him, so it's not relevant."

"Forgiveness comes from within." She patted her chest. "From here."

"Oh bless." I flipped open my laptop. "Tell you what, I'll search social media and see if I can find him. That way you can actually tell him you forgive him. What's his name again?"

She burst from her chair and slammed my laptop shut. "Don't you dare do that."

I smiled. "Point made." If I'd had a mirror on hand, I was pretty sure I'd see a glimmer or sparkle in my eye.

"Fine."

"Fine. Can we move on now, please?"

"Whatever." She marched back to her chair as if she'd actually won that argument.

"I'm going to see Sonny Waddell in a bit."

"Why?"

"Because I think he should know the land is rightfully his."

"Do you think it's going to matter now anyway? He's probably going to jail for the rest of his life."

"He's got kids. It'll probably matter to them."

"They'll probably just sell the land. I don't think they've been back in years."

"Then it'll matter to us."

"Good point," she said.

"I'm making a lot of those today, aren't I?"

She shot me a death stare, and I laughed. "When is his bail hearing?"

"I don't know, and I doubt Dylan will let me know either." I tossed a piece of paper onto the ground just to see if she'd pitch a fit.

"No comment."

"Probably best."

"Do you want me to send the information to the attorney and bidders?"

"I've got copies waiting for me at the office supply store, and I've already forwarded them the email, but I could use your help with that decluttering thing we're doing next month."

"Sure. What do you need?"

I forwarded her the class syllabus and the information I'd put together and gave her a few ideas of how I saw the class going. "Would you be able to get an email to our subscribers out? See if we can get anyone to sign up for it?"

"Yeah, no problem."

"I think doing a few of these kinds of things a year are great marketing opportunities for us, especially now that all these data hubs are moving further north of the city. I thought maybe we could put together a community yard sale or something, too. We could hold it at the high school and get them to help run it through the DECA program."

"Oh, I love that idea. I'll contact the school and see what I can do to set something up."

"Perfect. Have I told you how incredible you are lately?"

"You just did."

I gathered my things. "Okay, I'm out of here. Heading back to the office supply store and then to see Sonny Waddell."

"And very likely run into Dylan."

"Let's hope I don't."

"Let's hope you do," she whispered.

"I heard that," I said as I walked toward the door.

"I wanted you to, and by the way, don't think I don't know why you threw that paper on the ground. Now pick it up."

I marched back over to it and laughed as I threw it in the trash.

"Thank you."

* * *

Sonny wasn't all that happy to see me, but that didn't surprise me at all.

"What do you want?"

I dropped the papers from the office supply store on the table in front of me. The glass divider rested on the table so he could see what they were. "A few days ago I contacted the Georgia Historical Society about the original property lines for your land."

He didn't change the blank expression on his face, but he glanced down at the papers and back at me.

"You were right, at least for the most part. Someone changed the plot lines in the Pickett's favor." I pressed the legal-sized paper against the window. "But the Waddell's actually own more of the land than you thought. About another ten feet across and all the way to the end of the property." I yanked the paper away, leaned back in my seat and folded my hands across my chest. "Looks like you killed Jesse Pickett for nothing."

"I didn't kill that boy."

"I saw you leaving there, and I saw the shovel in your hand."

"I didn't kill that boy."

"You threatened him and you threatened me. How am I supposed to believe you?"

"Because I ain't no liar."

Says every killer on TV, I thought. "That's not good enough for me."

"Why would I kill him? That land don't belong to him anyway. Even you told me that. He just gets me all ticked off, and I shoot off at the mouth, that's all, but I didn't kill him."

He did have a point. He did know Jesse wasn't getting the land. His issue wasn't that as much as the land going to a builder. "If you didn't kill him, why did I see you leaving and why did I see you put that shovel against the house, and why did Dylan arrest you?"

He dragged his hand down his gray beard and tugged on its end. "'Cause I'm an idiot, that's why."

"I'm going to need something a little better than that."

"I heard some yelling over there, and I knew nobody was supposed to be there, so I went over to check things out."

He stopped talking. "And?"

"And that's when I found Jesse on the floor. The shovel was lying there next to him, and I don't know why, but I moved it out of the way when I checked to see if he was breathing. When I saw that he wasn't, I panicked, and I figured I better put it somewhere so they didn't think I did it, so that's what I did."

"The shovel had blood on it, Sonny."

"I wasn't really thinking clearly."

If he was telling the truth, that was obvious. "So, let me get this straight. You're saying you heard yelling at Myrtle's house, so you went over there and you found Jesse on the floor, dead, but you weren't sure he was dead, so when you went to check you unknowingly moved the murder weapon. When you realized you'd done that, you picked it up, laid it against the front porch window, and then went home?"

He nodded.

"Were you planning to call the sheriff?"

He stared at me, his jaw loose.

I raised an eyebrow. "Is that a no?"

"I don't really know what I was gonna do. Next thing I know, sheriff's at my house, and I'm here charged with murder."

His story was so unbelievable, I almost believed him. "Who would have killed him,

Sonny? The only other person invested in the property is you."

He shrugged. "I'm being framed. I didn't do it."

"Have you called your kids?"

He nodded. "My son is on his way now. Won't be here till tomorrow."

"Okay."

"Do you believe me?"

I gathered up the papers and put them in my bag. "I don't know Sonny. I just don't know."

As I left the Sheriff's Office, Dylan caught me in the parking lot. "Can we talk?"

"I have a lot to do. The property lines changed and that means the valuation on the property is different now, so I've got to do a new one, and that means a whole new sales price and listing, and I don't even know if the bidders are still in, and I've got to contact the attorney and the trust and find out what's going on." I rambled on without even making eye contact. "Maybe tomorrow. If I'm caught up, I guess."

He grabbed my arm, "Lily."

"Not now Dylan."

He didn't let go. "The judge is asking for the trust to indefinitely postpone the sale of the property. He wants to demolish the house and have the land excavated."

I stopped walking and finally turned around and made eye contact. "What? Why?"

"He's done. Said this old wives' tale needs to be put to an end."

"But he doesn't have that right."

"Actually, he does. I told him you have paperwork proving the original plot lines, and he wants to see them so the land belonging to the Waddell's isn't disturbed, but he's determined to make this happen."

"What does he think this is, the 1700s or something? He doesn't have to have the land excavated. Why wouldn't he use a radar survey company? They use those to find utility pipelines all the time." I recalled what Myrtle had said about the boxes in the attic and realized destroying the house meant I needed those boxes. "When is he planning to do this?"

"I'm not sure. He asked me to get a copy of the paperwork from you, so probably soon."

"Can I at least talk to him about it first?"

"You can, but I'm not sure he's going to change his mind."

"Digging is expensive. Who's paying for this? The county?"

"I think he's planning to hit the trust with the bill."

"What? He can't do that. That's not right. I'm calling the attorney. They'll file some kind of injunction or something. I don't know what, but they'll find a way to stop him. He can't do this."

"He all but owns this town, Lily. You know how it goes. Small town and a judge with a big ego. Do what you need to, but I've got to get that paperwork to him."

That big-ego could get a copy of the paperwork himself for all I cared. I glanced at my bag. "I don't have any with me at the moment. I'll have to get it to you later, but I really have to go."

"I'll need it by the end of the day," he said as I climbed into my car.

"I'll do my best." I had to get to Myrtle's and grab those few boxes in her attic before the judge did anything to the house. I didn't know what was in them, but I'd promised my client I'd do what she asked, and I intended to at least follow through with one of my promises.

* * *

Myrtle's place was completely trashed. I didn't know if Jesse had done the damage or whether others had come through and destroyed it, but a tornado wouldn't ruin a home to the level Myrtle's place had been. I sat on the only chair left standing in the kitchen and cried. "Who does this?"

The walls were smashed in all through the kitchen and family room. Hole after hole after hole filled them, leaving only tiny bits of wall visible. Upholstered furniture slashed through so much the stuffing lay on the floor next to it. I followed the path of destruction to the old woman's bedroom and found the same vandalism. Her bed, torn and shattered to pieces, her dresser drawers split apart and crushed. Clothes torn and shredded, lying all over.

Whoever did this wasn't searching for money. They intended to demolish, and from the looks of it, their intent was laced with anger.

But why?

Myrtle wasn't the nicest woman in town. Everyone knew that, but who hated her enough to mutilate everything the dead woman owned?

The person that killed her. Her great-nephew.

Was that what he was doing when Sonny heard the yelling? In a fit of rage, had Jesse come to his family home and destroyed what belonged to his aunt, the things he couldn't have? Had Sonny caught him and killed him? Was it an accident? If so, why didn't Sonny say so?

Because after the scene at Millie's, no one would believe him.

Even I hadn't.

I rushed up to the attic and grabbed the two small boxes poor Myrtle Redbecker had asked me to take care of if something happened to her, and I put them in my trunk for safe keeping and then headed home to finish up my work for the day.

I contacted the attorney handling the trust to discuss what Dylan told me. He wasn't sure of a specific precedent for a case like ours but said there had been many cases where a judge had postponed a sale over land disputes or inheritance issues. "He could in some way attach his ruling to one of these precedents and demand the property be excavated to stop any potential future lawsuits."

I groaned. "But what about charging the trust, and can't we do anything about the excavation? He can use a utility line locating company. This is what they do. Can't you suggest it? It's a lot less expensive. Maybe if we go to him with that option he'll consider it?"

"I'll approach the judge about it. In the meantime, though, we'll need to officially take the property off the market."

"Thank you. Do you want to contact the bidders then, or should I?"

"Since I get paid from the trust and you're commissioned, I can do it."

"I'd appreciate it. I'll swing by and grab the key box and the sign, oh, and I'll take it offline also."

"Sounds good," he said.

That's because you're still getting paid, I thought, but I didn't say anything.

"By the way, Mrs. Redbecker asked that you be paid a fee if the deal didn't close. Would you like me to send you the check, or should I have it deposited to your account?"

After I picked my jaw up off the floor, I gave him the business account information. Maybe old cantankerous Myrtle Redbecker wasn't such a crank after all.

Chapter Seven

My adorable little bungalow felt less adorable without Sparky, even though I'd never even met the dog, and he'd never once stepped foot into the place. If Belle were there at that moment I would have punched her in the shoulder for putting the idea of a puppy into my head. Not that I would rather think about the death toll rising in my small town, or the fact that my ex-boyfriend had moved back and seemed to want me back, too, but I would have preferred to think about something less heart wrenching.

Maybe I'd get a fish?

Yes. A fish. That would definitely do the trick. A fish wasn't high maintenance. A fish didn't require too much time or effort, they didn't need to be walked, or trained. I didn't have to take a fish to the vet. They couldn't get hit by cars or require kenneling if I went on vacation—which I never did, but whatever. Fish were easy. Fish fit into my lifestyle.

I was totally getting a fish. STAT.

I threw on a pair of yoga pants and a sweatshirt and headed back to the next town over and the big box pet store next to the office supply store. Instead of heading straight to the fish aisle, my heart aimed right at the dog section, and I found myself wandering around the puppy items. I draped my hand across a leather leash, a soft dog bed made out of some plush plaid material and an assortment of cushioned, squeaky toys with Sparky's name written in invisible ink all over them.

I hated Belle for planting the puppy seed in my brain.

I dragged myself kicking and screaming over to the fish section but nothing spoke to my heart the way the puppy supplies did, and I had to believe a fish wasn't in my future. Not that a puppy was either but a fish definitely wasn't.

I left the store empty handed and even more broken hearted. I hoped whoever adopted that sweet Sparky treated him like the king I knew he'd grow up to be.

I took the scenic route home, driving past Myrtle's place to check on it just to make myself feel better. I didn't go inside, but from the outer appearance, nothing had changed. I hadn't said anything to Dylan about going there earlier, figuring he'd be upset and that he'd already known the house had been trashed anyway. Mostly I didn't have the strength to talk to him and figured if I didn't, he couldn't press me about the paperwork. I hoped the attorney for the trust had already spoken to the judge, and I didn't need to worry about getting him the paperwork. If he still wanted it bad enough he could serve me with papers or get them from the Historical Society himself. Only when I finally pulled into my driveway, Dylan's sheriff's car was parked there waiting for me. I gave up and decided to just give Dylan the papers and let the attorney fight it out with the judge. As much as I wanted to do right by my client, the legal component wasn't my area of expertise, and the rumors of the buried money wasn't my battle to fight.

I locked my car and walked toward my side door. "I have the papers inside. I'll grab them for you."

He opened his car door and stepped out of the car.

"You're not coming in, so don't bother getting out." I didn't need to check his facial expression. I felt the shock of my words vibrate through the air.

"Okay."

I unlocked the door and went to grab the papers from my bag on the table, only my bag wasn't on my table. I checked the floor, but it wasn't there either. I made a quick search through my standard bag drops throughout my small bungalow, but my bag wasn't there. I knew I brought it home. I'd had it with me all day, and I'd definitely had it with me when I saw Sonny and spoke to Dylan last because I specifically avoided giving him the paperwork then, and I'd come straight home and done some work, tossed everything back into it for the morning and put it back on the table.

So where was it?

Dylan knocked on my side door. "Can I come in?" he asked as he opened the door. He must have noticed the frown on my face. "I just need the papers and I'll go. I promise."

"I don't have them."

"Don't be like this Lily, please."

"No, I'm serious. I don't have them. My bag, it's gone." I did a circle in the room. "It was here before I left, but now it's gone." The hair on my arms stood. "I think someone was in my house again."

Dylan placed his hand on his gun and whispered, "Get in your car and drive down to the end of the street. Now."

"But—"

He cut me off. "Now."

He pulled his gun from the holster on his waist. "I'll come find you."

Before I had time to argue a loud bang and crash boomed from the front of my house. The front door slammed shut, and the sound of someone running echoed outside. Dylan took off running out my side door. I didn't know what to do, so I followed him, but bless him, those spin classes were no match to his cardiovascular capabilities, and I couldn't keep up. He raced past the sidewalk and to the right, and within seconds I'd lost sight of him and the shadow of whomever he chased.

I bent over, hands on my knees and forced myself to breathe. All I could think about was how Sparky would have been able to catch whomever was in my house but a dang fish would have been utterly useless, and I fell to the ground laughing because of it.

Dylan came back and stood over me, watching me as I laughed. "You okay?"

I couldn't speak, the laughter taking over, probably masking a ton of emotions I just couldn't deal with at that moment. "I…I…" I nodded since I couldn't finish my sentence.

He dropped my bag on the ground next to me. "Here. They left this on the side of the road." He sat next to me, leaned back onto the palms of his hands, his legs spread straight out in front of him. "Whoever that was ought to be in the Olympics."

I opened my bag, but my laptop and the file with the paperwork were both gone. "Now I definitely don't have the paperwork for the judge."

He peeked into my bag. "Anything else missing?"

"My laptop."

"Crap."

"Yeah. Luckily I'm smart enough to keep everything backed up at work. I can at least get him a copy of the email in the morning."

"I'd appreciate that. He can be nasty when he wants. I'd rather not get on his bad side."

"Like that Vicki Lawrence song?"

"The one your mother used to sing all the time? Yeah."

"You remember that?"

"I remember a lot of things."

"Me, too." Dang. A weak moment.

"What did you have in that bag that someone might want?"

I thought about that for a minute. "I don't think anything." I zipped up the large compartment and set the bag to my side. "Do you think this has something to do with the plot lines?"

"Are you involved in any other murder investigations or land disputes or any small town family feuds?"

I couldn't help but smile. "Not that I'm aware of."

"Then I think it's safe to say this has something to do with Myrtle Redbecker's property."

"But what? And how? Jesse Pickett is dead, and his killer is in jail."

"I have a feeling there's something going on that we're both missing."

"So, how do we find out what that is?"

"We don't. That's my job. Your job is selling real estate."

"And I can't do that because people keep getting killed at my listing. Which, by the way, isn't even my listing anymore."

"You have other clients."

"Not ones that would have made my office close to fifty thousand bucks."

"Ouch."

"I know, right?"

"Doesn't Odell Luna want to sell now?"

"Do you think Odell—"

"Stay out of it Lily, please. You just had someone enter your home again, and this time you were in it. You could have been killed." He stood and wiped the grass from his pants. "In fact, I'm not comfortable with you staying alone. I'm staying on your couch tonight."

I jumped up. "Uh, I don't think so. I can stay with Belle."

"Fine. You go to Belle's, but I'm staying here. Whoever came here is looking for something and if it wasn't in your bag, they might show up again, and I'm going to be here." He walked to his car. "In fact, I think it's a good idea for you to go to Belle's place."

"I'm not comfortable with someone staying at my place without me."

He flipped around and stared at me. "Lily, it's me," he stressed me with extra intensity.

"I don't care if it's the Pope. It makes me uncomfortable."

"The Pope I can understand. You're not even Catholic, but this is me we're talking about, and I'm the sheriff here. What do you think I'm going to do, snoop through old love letters?"

"No" I mumbled the rest. "The only ones you'd find are the ones from you anyway."

The side of his mouth twitched, darn it. "You still have my old letters?"

"If I had them, I mean." Great. Just great. "You're not staying here without me. That's just creepy."

"Fine, you can stay too, but I want you in your room with the door locked in case something happens, and I'll check your window to make sure it's secure."

"As if I'd keep the door unlocked with you're here anyway."

His mouth twitched again and my heart melted. I'd all but forgotten about poor Sparky.

He opened his trunk and removed a travel bag. "I keep an extra set of clothes in the car for emergencies."

I couldn't help but wonder how many similar emergencies he'd had as a cop, but I knew I really didn't want to know.

* * *

The next morning Belle showed up at the office with two lavender scones. "Are you going to stay mad at me forever?"

"Maybe." I'd already forgotten why I was mad at her, and that I had been in the first place, but I wanted that scone, so I pretended otherwise.

"Can't we let bygones be bygones?"

I broke off a piece of the creamy warm yumminess and handed it to my best friend. "My old maid-ness is forever over."

Her eyes widened. "Do tell."

"I had a man over last night."

"Honey, you are a southern girl. We do not misbehave like that." She pulled her chair to my desk. "Now, give me every single detail, and then go straight to church and beg for forgiveness."

"A southern girl doesn't kiss and tell."

She dropped her head and shook it. "Well, that's a big downer. Thanks for that."

"Sorry, but I did have a man spend the night."

"Did one of your brothers come in town or something?"

"Nice. No, it was our sheriff, actually."

She raised a finger to her partially opened mouth. "Oh yeah, now I'm dying to know."

"I'd gone to the pet store to buy a fish, and when I got home he was there waiting." I stopped just to torture her.

"A fish?"

"Long story."

"Okay. Tell me that part later."

"Apparently, the sale of Myrtle's property is officially on hold now. The judge is pushing to excavate the land and tear the house down. He's determined to put a stop to everything related to the money rumor, and he needs the paperwork from the Georgia Historical Society, so Dylan came to get it."

"What? That's ridiculous, and expensive. Why isn't he just using a utility locating service to search for it?"

"That's exactly what I said. Anyway, so, I went inside to grab the paperwork from my bag, but my bag was gone. Dylan came in and we heard someone running out the front door and—"

"Wait, someone was in your house?"

"Yes, and Dylan raced after them, and he's really fast, but he didn't catch them. They dropped my bag, but my computer and the file with the paperwork were gone, and he didn't want me to stay home, so he told me I had to go to your house, but I didn't want him staying at my house alone, so—"

"Oh goodness, I hope you did not sleep with him. You'll be the talk of the town if that gets out."

I smacked her arm. "No, he slept on the couch, and I slept in my room. With the door locked."

"Good. You definitely do not want to give him the milk for free. You most certainly want him to purchase the cow first."

"Did you just call me a cow?"

"Theoretically speaking, yes."

"So, let me get this straight. When you thought I would never date again, I was at risk of becoming an old maid, and just now, when you thought I might have slept with my former true love, you implied that I was easy and also that I was a cow?"

She cringed. "It sounds so tacky when you say it like that."

"It's actually horrible."

"But, really, I'm just concerned about your reputation." She brushed a hair from the side of her face. "And the reputation of our agency, of course, but only a little."

"Em hmm."

She laughed. "So, anyway, what happened after that?"

"Oh, I got up early and had my way with him on the couch, what did you think?"

She choked on a bite of her scone, and it took her almost a full minute to gather her composure.

I tried with all my might to keep a straight face, but I couldn't do it. "I'm kidding. He made a pot of coffee, and I came to work."

"So, now what?"

"Now I find new real estate clients, and we do our jobs."

"That's not what I mean, and you know it."

"I know, but I don't really have an answer, at least not about the personal stuff. The other stuff, I'm not sure. He's taken my statement, and he's filing a report, but really, what else can he do? I forwarded him the email from the Historical Society from my phone so he can give it to the judge, and I ordered a replacement laptop, which I can pick up at the office supply store today by the way, and he's got extra eyes—his term—on my place for now, so we'll see what happens."

"Aren't you worried? Someone broke into your house. Again."

I plucked a pencil from the holder and tapped it on the corner of my desk. "That's the thing. They didn't exactly break in. Or at least it doesn't look that way."

"Then how are they getting in?"

"I guess I'm leaving my door unlocked."

She shook her head. "Nope. No way. You're the last person that would do that. You still double check the door here when either one of us locks it. They're getting in somehow. You and Dylan just haven't figured out how yet."

"I'm not that obsessive, am I?"

"You used to mom all the girls in the sorority house, remember? Making sure everyone's straighteners were turned off before they left their rooms? You're totally obsessive."

"You're right. Someone is getting into my place somehow."

"Why don't you get an electronic doorbell? We're always telling our clients to get them. Maybe you should? I bet Dylan would install it, too."

The last thing I needed was him coming over to help me with anything. "I can do it myself."

"Whatever, I just think it's a good idea."

"Actually, I think you're right."

"Now if you'd only agree to the puppy." She put her hands together in a praying position. "Please? He's so cute."

"He's also so no longer at the shelter."

She gasped. "What? How do you know?"

"Because in a moment of weakness my car drove itself there and checked, and the nasty woman there said they'd let someone else adopt him."

A slow, knowing smile spread across Belle's face. "I knew it. I totally called it."

"You know nothing, and you called nothing, so hush."

"You wanted that dog. I can't believe you went to get him and he was gone. That really stinks."

"No, it just proves it wasn't meant to be. Besides, I decided I'm more of a fish girl instead, so that's what I'm getting. I just don't know what kind yet. I had no idea there were so many fish breeds to choose from. It's a big decision to make, and I don't want to rush my decision."

She rolled her eyes. "Whatever."

"Anyway, back to things that make money for us. Were you able to get anything together for the community garage sale and finish up the stuff for the decluttering class?"

She nodded. "What do you think I do while you're out and about with your ex-boyfriend?"

"Nice."

She giggled. "Everything's set for the class. I've even got Heather Barrington and Caroline Abernathy signed up. It should be entertaining to say the least."

"Dear Lord. You did not."

Belle struggled to maintain a straight face. "What? We finished college years ago. They can't still hate Savannah."

"Savannah stole and then married Heather's college boyfriend, the one she thought she was going to marry."

"Yeah, but she's divorcing him now, so maybe they'll make up."

"Right. Like that will ever happen." I rubbed the base of my neck. "And what about Caroline? Savannah slept with her boyfriend in college too."

Belle pointed at me. "That was never actually verified."

"God bless. You're going to send me to an early grave."

"Maybe, but the trip there will be a ton of fun!"

With a best friend like Belle, there was no doubt about that at all.

* * *

I couldn't understand how the world functioned before technology. Just a few hours laptopless and I'd just about lost my mind. My patience gone and my frustration level at a record high, I decided I needed a spin class and possibly even a yoga class just in case. Actually, the yoga class was Belle's idea, though she thought it was a long shot in the helping me regain my sanity department. I sort of leaned that direction too, but I at least wanted to attempt to remain open minded.

The next spin class wasn't for another thirty minutes, but I didn't care. I got my favorite bike set up, put my headphones on and played my personal spin playlist and did a quick twenty-minute workout before the room filled up for the next class. I finished out the hour long class too, but instead of following along to the instructors recommended intensity levels, I kicked mine up higher hoping to relieve the anxiety rushing through my veins.

By the time I completed a full eighty minutes of bike riding I was too exhausted to feel anything but the sweat pouring from my body. It would have been gross if I had any energy left to care.

I showered off at the gym, tossed on the clothes I'd arrived in and headed through town to the Dollar Plus store. I still needed the shower squeegee, which I'd been reminded of by the thin layer of soapy scum on the gym's shower walls. Aside from that, I had a mild curiosity about whatever might be happening between Junior Goodson and Grace Jeffers. I suspected it wasn't much more than a mild flirtation and really, it wasn't my business, but my curiosity got the best of me. I guess I needed something to distract myself from the events of the past few days. Besides, it was sort of on the way to get my new laptop anyway.

Sheila Jeffers was stocking a shelf full of deodorant as I walked into the store. "Well hiya, how are you?" Her smile consumed the entire bottom half of her face.

"Hi, Ms. Jeffers. I'm good. How are you?"

"I'm just peachy, you here to shop today or to see Grace again?"

I tinkered with the spray perfume bottles down the aisle from her. They smelled like cheap imitations of the expensive designer perfumes all the sorority girls wore at UGA. I preferred a simple body lotion scent over the heavy aroma of perfume any day. "Actually, a little of both. I'm looking for a window squeegee. Do you have those?"

She pushed herself up from the floor, moaning a bit in the process. "Sure do." She crooked her finger for me to follow. "Come this way. They're in the auto section."

I hadn't realized Dollar Plus had an auto section.

I followed her to the back of the store, near the laundry detergent aisle. Next to the car wash soap hung an assortment of clothes, sponges and squeegees. I picked the medium sized one. "Thank you. I need it for my shower at home. It's the easiest way to keep it clean." I hated making small talk. "How's Grace doing? Is she feeling better about Mrs. Redbecker?"

She nodded. "Seems to be fine. That girl's barely around much these days. You know how it is with teenagers. Comes and goes as she pleases. I can barely catch a glimpse of her these days."

"Maybe she's got a boyfriend keeping her busy?" I would never make it as a detective. I stunk at dropping hints to get someone to talk.

She laughed. "My Gracie? Not a chance. I raised her not to make the same mistakes as me. She's going places with that voice of hers.

She's got one of them YouTube channels with videos of her singing on them and is trying to get herself discovered." She tipped back on her heels. "I used to have a voice like that, but all those years of smoking did me in. Now I sound like I got me a frog stuck in my throat."

I wasn't sure what I was supposed to say to that. "I think that's great that she's trying to make a career of her singing. Is she back with the Meals Made for You program?"

We walked back to the cash register where Sheila checked me out.

"Nope. She decided to stop. Said it hurts too much when the people die."

"I understand. It can be hard when you have relationships with them."

"She's a kind-hearted soul. She don't take death lightly." She put my squeegee in a bag and handed it to me.

"I don't think anyone does. Thank you for the squeegee. Tell Grace I said hi and tell her good luck with her singing for me."

"Thanks, I'll do that."

Maybe Grace did have something going on with Junior Goodson, and she just didn't want her mother to know about it.

CHAPTER EIGHT

"Thank God, and thank you for letting me know."

"Who was that?" Belle asked.

"The attorney. He said the judge agreed to drop the excavation idea entirely."

"So he's going with the utility locating company instead?"

"Nope. He's dropping the whole idea completely."

"Really? That's incredible. Why?"

"Because this attorney rocks, that's why. He said doing so could potentially open up the idea that every old wives' tale could wind up a lawsuit and tie up the judge's schedule for years. I guess he had his paralegal do a little quick research and found a few cases to support his argument, and the judge agreed that could open a Pandora's Box, so he nixed it completely."

"We are so using this attorney for everything."

"He's not exactly a closing attorney."

"Well, he should be."

"So, is the land back on the market?"

"Almost. He's preparing the paperwork to refile the corrected property lines now. Since it's been considered the Pickett property for so long, legally it can be argued to be theirs, but since it was illegally acquired, the judge said he'll sign off on reinstating it back to the Waddell family. Once the forms are filled out and refiled, we're good to go. Should be a few days if not sooner."

"Is this guy single?"

"The attorney?"

She nodded.

"I don't know, but he's probably at least fifty, so…"

"Hey, I'm asking for you, not me."

"I'm getting a fish. I don't need a boyfriend."

"Yeah, because those two are even remotely similar."

Because he had perfect timing, Dylan coughed then, startling both of us.

"When did you walk in?" I asked.

"Just before you compared owning a fish to having a relationship." The side of his mouth twitched.

"That's not exactly what I said."

"Pretty close," Belle interjected.

I glared at her.

She blanched.

"Anyway," I tried to sound professional. "what can we do for you, Sheriff?"

He removed his hat as he walked closer to our desks. "Thought I'd let you know Sonny's bail hearing is tomorrow morning."

"I'll bring the popcorn," Belle said.

Dylan laughed. "Sounds about right for this town."

"What are the odds he'll even get it?"

"My guess is pretty low," Dylan said.

"I figured."

Belle agreed. "He seems pretty volatile. If it was up to me, I wouldn't let him out either."

"Which is why you're in real estate and not law," I said.

"What's that supposed to mean?"

"It's innocent before proven guilty, not the other way around, remember?"

"Not according to the social media."

Dylan and I exchanged a familiar glance—the one we used to share all the time when Belle said something we both thought was ridiculous. It tugged at my heart strings, and I caught the moment he realized what we'd done too, because he looked away and down. That didn't tug at my heart strings. It yanked those things right out.

I forced myself to refocus by shuffling papers on my desk and talk about the case. "So, what do you think?"

He raised his right brow.

"Do you think he killed Myrtle Redbecker or do you still think Jesse did that?"

He placed his hat on his head and maneuvered it gently from side to sit until it fit just right. There was a certain science to a man placing his head into a well-fitted suede or leather hat. Dylan had mastered it and watching him was sheer pleasure.

"Sonny Waddell is charged with killing Jesse Pickett, not Myrtle Redbecker."

"So, you still think Jesse killed his great aunt?"

He just gave me a blank-faced expression as a response.

"Did you check the note against any writing samples like I suggested?"

He exhaled. "The District Attorney and I are still evaluating the two murders. We're still interviewing Waddell. His attorney isn't allowing him to answer any questions about Myrtle Redbecker."

"That means his attorney knows he did it," I said.

He straightened his stance, pushing his shoulders back just a touch. "No, that means his attorney doesn't want him saying anything that might make us think one way or the other. They don't want us to know anything to lead us in any direction. They want us off balance."

"Sounds like he's got a good attorney," Belle said.

He nodded. "His son hired someone from an Atlanta firm. One of the best in the Southeast apparently."

She laughed. "Judge is going to love that."

"Judge is going to rip him apart," I mumbled.

Dylan chuckled. "Poor guy won't know what hit him."

"Exactly." I asked if he knew about the excavating decision, but he didn't.

"Glad to hear it worked out that way."

"Why won't you tell me who you think killed Myrtle?" I asked.

"Because what I think doesn't matter, Lily. It's what the evidence shows that's important, and the evidence still shows Jesse Pickett killed his aunt."

"Then you're not looking at the right evidence."

"I can only look at the evidence I have."

"I guess."

We finished up with small talk, but I couldn't let go of the thought that something wasn't right. I just wasn't sure what it was.

* * *

That night I went home with a brand new electronic video doorbell and new door locks. I purchased metal rods cut to the size of my windows—when closed—to brace between the top of the frame and the top of the closed window itself to stop anyone from opening them. I switched out every door lock, secured every window, and installed the new video doorbell system in two hours and then decided to celebrate my success by relaxing outside with a freshly made glass of sweet iced tea and the newest release by my favorite thriller author.

As good of a writer as she was, I just couldn't get into the story. Regardless of the locks and metal bars, I just didn't feel safe in my own home. Nothing I did gave me any peace of mind, and nothing allowed me to relax. I paced the length of my small back yard, mentally attempting to connect the unconnected dots of both murders together. The neighbor's dog barked, and I jumped. Something rustled the tree branches toward the back of my yard and startled me enough to send me in a near sprint to the light by my back door. It would have made me laugh, but my uncontrollable teeth chattering pushed me over my limit.

I texted Belle. "Can I stay at your place tonight?"

"Um, is everything okay?"

"Yes, but I just don't feel right at my place. I don't feel safe."

"Why don't you call Dylan and have him stay again?"

"Because I don't want him staying here."

"Okay. You can stay at my place, but I'm not going to be home tonight. I'm in the ATL."

"I don't want to stay alone. You're in Atlanta?"

"Yes."

"When did you go there?"

"Right after I left the office."

"And you're coming back when?"

"What's with the twenty questions?" she texted back.

"You're with a guy, aren't you?"

"Maybe."

"Why haven't you told me about this?"

"I'm not staying with him. I'm staying at a hotel. I didn't want you getting the wrong idea."

"I don't have the wrong idea, and that's not what I meant anyway." I sent the text and then dialed her number, but it went to voicemail. "Why aren't you answering?" I texted.

"Because I'm with a guy, remember?"

"Oh, right. What I meant was, why didn't you tell me about him?"

"I wanted to wait until I decided how I feel."

"Have you decided?"

"I think so."

"And?"

"And I'll tell you when I see you."

I yelped. "Ugh. Fine." I texted the angry-faced emoji and tapped on it several times just to make sure she knew I meant it.

She responded with the angel emoji. As if. "Are you going to stay at my place?"

"Probably not. It's not the same if you're not there."

"Well, if you change your mind, you know where I hide the key."

"Thanks."

Wait a minute. That was it. I hid a key too. Maybe whoever got into my house knew where I'd hidden my key. I made a beeline to the flower pot on the right side of my garage and pushed it up on its side. The key was missing. I let out a breath and then released it when I remembered I'd given the key to the plumber last week and was supposed to pick it up already.

Whoever got into my house was doing it without a key, and without breaking a window or a lock. So, how could they get in? I knew if I had that answer I'd be able to figure out who got into my house, and if I knew who that was, I'd know who killed Myrtle. I also believed that whoever killed Myrtle killed Jesse.

I needed to see that note again. If Dylan didn't plan to have the writing analyzed, maybe I could try and analyze it myself. Not to the degree of a professional, of course, but I knew the difference between feminine writing and masculine writing at least, and I had access to the Internet. I could at least take a wild guess if the note had been penned by an older person or someone nearer to my age. Maybe. If nothing else it was at least worth a shot.

That meant I'd have to see Dylan. But at least I wouldn't have to be alone, and I wouldn't be asking him to be with me because I was scared. I bit the bullet and made the call.

"Hey Lily, what's up?"

"Do you think you could bring the note by?"

"The note?"

"The one left at my house? I'd like to take another look at it."

"It's evidence in an open case, Lily."

"An open case involving my house."

"That's not the point."

"What exactly is the point?"

He groaned. "Why do you want to see the note?"

It was my turn to groan. "It may not matter a whole lot to you, but I don't feel all that safe in my house right now, and this is my home, Dylan. The one place I should feel safe."

"I'll be there in a bit."

"Thank you."

Fifteen minutes later he knocked on my door, note, a frozen pizza and a bag of kettle chips in hand. "This was the best I could do with such short notice."

I smiled. "You never were much of a chef."

"Hey, I tried."

I opened the bag of chips and dumped them into a plastic bowl. "Points for that."

He set the oven to preheat. "At least you're giving me credit for something."

"Can you set the timer, too?" I smiled when he did it without missing a beat. "And, by the way, I've given you credit for a lot of things."

"Name one."

I had to think about that. "When you put me on the spot like this, I can't come up with anything."

"Because you haven't given me any credit, but it's okay. I kind of deserve it."

"I'm not going to argue that."

He laid the note on the table, flattening out the baggie we'd stored it in. "Well? What say you?"

I sat at the table and examined the note carefully. *Make sure that property don't sell or else.*

"Obviously a man wrote it."

He put the pizza in the oven and then sat next to me. "What makes you think that?"

"Because most women don't abuse the English language like that."

"You're in the South. We have our own version of the English language here."

"That's true. Let me rephrase that then. Most females my age don't talk like that."

"Then who does?"

"Old school southerners, people who've lived here all their lives, maybe ones who don't have a lot of education. Those reality show people."

He laughed. "I think they're actually acting."

"Bless. I sure hope so."

"But you've got a point. So, think about what you're saying. Who do you know involved in this investigation that fits into any of those?" He went to the oven and peeked inside. "It's got another minute or two."

"The timer will go off when it's done." I knew where he was going, and I didn't want to answer his question. "But it could be a cover up, too."

He nodded. "It could be. You watch crime shows though, and you know how it goes. Most criminals aren't that smart. So, tell me, who do you know involved in this investigation fits into any of those options?"

"Practically the whole town fits into at least one of those."

"My point exactly."

"That's why you should have the handwriting analyzed." I flipped the note sideways. "I mean, seriously. It's block letters, so it's obviously a male."

"Females only write in cursive?"

"Well, no."

"So, a woman wouldn't specifically write in block letters to throw the cops off?"

"Maybe, but—you're just validating my point. Why not get a hand writing analysis done? Whoever did this obviously killed Myrtle too."

"What makes you think that?"

"Because of the cast iron skillet."

"What about it?"

"Myrtle was killed with hers, and the note was left in mine."

"Billy Ray basically announced to the entire town the weapon used to kill Myrtle. That doesn't mean the person that killed her left the note."

Dang it. He was right. "But why would someone be so cruel?"

"Because someone doesn't want that property to sell bad enough to scare you into taking it off the market. So, tell me, who would that be?"

"Sonny Waddell."

He gave me a single head nod just as the oven dinged letting us know the pizza was done.

"And Sonny still could have killed Myrtle. I don't know why you can't see that."

"May I have a piece of paper and a pen?"

I directed him to the desk drawer while I got the pizza out and cut us both slices. We each ate while Dylan wrote out a chart listing Sonny Waddell and Jesse Pickett's possible motives for Myrtle's murder and the evidence surrounding each of them.

Seeing it on paper hit me in an unexpected way. "Wow."

"What?"

"Based on this, either one of them could have done it."

"But Jesse had more to lose."

"I disagree."

"Why?"

"Because he'd already lost it. He was just hoping to get it back. He felt it should stay in the family, and he wanted it, but he knew she'd taken it from him. Sonny on the other hand, his family had fought for years for that land, and he was determined to keep fighting for it. He made that perfectly clear. He said the land belonged to him." I took a bite of my slice of pizza and spoke with my mouth full. If my momma had been there, she would have kicked me under the table. "Jesse was a defeated man. Sonny prepared for battle."

He put down his slice of pizza. "You really think Sonny killed Myrtle Redbecker don't you?"

"I don't want to think it, but yes, I do."

He focused on the chart. "I can talk to the District Attorney, but I don't know what that'll get me." He picked up the note and stared at it. "The least I can do is push for no bail."

"You'd do that for me?"

He angled his body toward mine. Our knees touched, and I didn't, or more like I couldn't, move. "I can't think of anything I wouldn't do for you."

I swallowed hard.

He leaned forward, and I leaned forward, and I swallowed hard again. He wanted to kiss me, and I wanted to kiss him, too. I wanted it more than I'd ever wanted anything, but I couldn't. I just couldn't. I tilted my head down and to the right. "I can't. I'm sorry." I stood. "You…you should go."

He held up his cell phone. "I'm not leaving."

I read the text message on his phone. "She didn't."

He nodded. "She's worried about you."

Belle sent him a text asking him to stay with me for the night since she wasn't in town. "I'm a big girl. I can take care of myself."

He showed me another text. It was a screenshot of my text messages to Belle.

"She's a traitor."

"She's your best friend."

"Still a traitor. You can't stay here. You just—we just—"

"We won't."

"You're right. We won't, but it's—"

"I'm not leaving." He walked out my kitchen door, grabbed his bag from his trunk, and came back. "Besides, your couch is comfy."

I rolled my eyes. "Fine. One night."

"One night." The corner of his mouth twitched. "For now."

I flipped around, tossed the empty frozen pizza box into the garbage and marched off to make up the couch for him without saying another word.

* * *

The next morning he'd made coffee and left before I had the guts to come out of my bedroom. He did leave me a note telling me Sonny's bail hearing was set for ten o'clock. He scheduled a meeting with the District Attorney and hoped to convince him to push for no bail. Given that Sonny's attorney was a big Atlanta one, I thought no bail was a long shot but hoped for the best anyway.

Belle and I exchanged texts, neither offering a ton of explicit details about our nights—sort of—with men, but I knew we'd have a lot of catching up to do later. In the meantime, I followed up with some business housekeeping and headed straight to the courthouse/jail along with the rest of the town to see what happened with Sonny Waddell.

Millie, Old Man Goodson and Odell Luna stood next to me in the long line to get inside.

"Looks like we're all itching to see the big event," Old Man Goodson said.

"This stuff's better than what's on the TV these days," Odell Luna said.

Millie nudged my shoulder and winked at me. "Now you two, don't be like that. I know your momma's taught you better manners than that."

Both men straightened their shoulders and didn't make eye contact with Millie. I did, but I had to look away quickly so I wouldn't laugh.

Odell straightened his shirt. "Lilybit, I still want to sell my property. Belle got me that paperwork. Think you can come by sometime before the weekend and explan it to me? Or, if you like, I can bring it by your office. Whatever works?"

"I'm happy to come by your place and get it, Odell. I'll have to take a few pictures and get some additional information from you anyway. Later this morning work for you?"

He nodded. "That'll be fine."

"Great."

Belle finally made it back and cut in line next to me. We chatted briefly with Millie and then Belle whispered in my ear. "I swear something's up with them." She pointed to the couple scurrying away from us.

I saw the back of Junior Goodson and what I thought was Grace Jeffers push through the crowd and disappear. "Was that who I think it was?"

She nodded.

"Maybe he's helping her with her YouTube videos?"

"Right. That's what they're doing." She made a face that led me to believe that wasn't what she thought they were doing at all.

"Ew. Stop."

"Well, come on."

Dylan stepped outside and spoke into a megaphone. "May I have your attention, please?"

The crowd quieted instantly.

"Due to the nature of this investigation, and an agreement made between the district attorney, Mr. Waddell, his attorney, and Judge Bennett, there will be no bail hearing today. You all can go home."

It took a second, but only that before the crowd buzzed with questions.

"What's going on?"

"Is Sonny guilty?"

"Did he confess?"

"Is the judge going to hang him?"

What was that even?

"When is the hearing going to be?"

Dylan picked a few of the questions to answer. "No, Sonny Waddell is not going to be hanged. This is 2018. We haven't had a trial to determine guilt or innocence, and he's yet to state whether he's guilty or innocent as his attorney has not allowed him to speak. We are not having a hearing as all involved have agreed that Mr. Waddell will remain incarcerated until trial. Thank you.

More questions shot out from the crowd.

"When is the trial?"

"What about the property? Can we start checking for the money now?"

I wasn't sure who yelled that, but the voice sounded familiar.

A few more questions came before Dylan's hand flew up. "People, please. Once we have a date, I'm sure we'll make an announcement. The property is privately owned, if anyone steps foot on it and tries to dig a hole in it or even comes close to it with a shovel, I'll throw you in jail for trespassing. You understand? Now go on, get out of here. Don't you have to be at work or something anyway? This town can't function without you all working."

The group let out a collective sign and a few dropped their popcorn, which caused Dylan to threaten them with littering fines, and finally everyone but Belle and I left.

"You knew that would happen, didn't you?" I asked.

"What, the littering?"

"No, the no bail thing."

"I was about eighty percent sure."

"Did you add Myrtle's death to the charges?"

"Not yet, but I think the District Attorney is headed that direction. He's considering offering a plea for a double confession."

"Wow. You've got the crime speak down well," Belle said.

Dylan smirked. "I hope so. It's my job."

"Oh, yeah. Well, I hadn't really thought of it that way."

"Does the District Attorney think he killed Myrtle?"

"It would appear so."

I felt a sense of relief flood over me. "Then I guess I'm safe to be home alone again."

"I'm happy to stay one more night if you think you need me to."

"No, I'm good. Thank you though."

We stood in awkward silence for what seemed like an eternity. Dylan finally broke it.

"So, Matt says things are going well," he said to Belle.

My mouth dropped. "Matt? Who's—wait. Is that the guy you went out with last night?" I pointed to Dylan. "How do you—oh my gosh." I flipped back toward Belle. "He set you up with the guy, didn't he? And you didn't tell me?"

A flush of bright red crept up Belle's neck and across her cheeks. "No, I mean, yes, but for business, not pleasure. It sounds bad when you say it like that."

My stomach clenched. "It feels bad when I say it. I can't believe you didn't tell me."

"It's not a big deal," Dylan said. "I'm looking for a Deputy Sheriff and Matt's looking to get out of Atlanta, so I asked Belle to meet him and tell him about Bramblett County. She was going to be in the city anyway, so she said she'd meet him there."

"Yeah, and we—I don't know, I guess we just kind of hit it off, so we went out again. Last night. And it was fun. It wasn't like a set up or anything. Not really."

"He must have liked you because he's taking the job."

Belle's eyes sparkled. "I know, isn't that great?"

"You'll like him," Dylan said to me. "He's a good guy. We all should go out for dinner when he gets to town."

"Definitely. It'll be like old times," Belle said.

"Only this time Dylan and I aren't dating," I reminded her.

"Well, there is that," she said.

More awkward silence. "Okay then, I've got to run. People to see, places to go and all," I said.

"Okay. I'll see you at the office in a bit?" Belle asked.

"I'll be there."

I smiled at Dylan. "Thank you for doing what you did."

He returned the smile and tipped his head. "Of course."

CHAPTER NINE

I'd received a voicemail from the trust attorney earlier that morning saying we were good to go with Myrtle's property again. Unfortunately, two of the bidders had backed out, and both were the highest bids, so he wanted to relist the property. I'd kept the key box and for sale items in my car, so, I decided I'd stop there after seeing Odell Luna and put everything back up and check on the property just to make sure it wasn't any more destroyed than before. I'd heard rumors of people going there in the night and digging for the money, even entering the home and damaging it further, but what was done was done, and

Myrtle was already dead, so I had to let it go. I'd removed the two boxes she'd asked me to keep safe and at some point, I'd get to the bank to get that letter from the safety deposit box and do what it said.

Odell answered the door right away. "Howdy Lilybit, I was wondering when you'd get here. Just fixed a new batch of sweet tea. Want some?"

"It's toasty outside, so that would be great. Thank you."

I reviewed the paperwork with Odell, gave him a detailed walk through the process, and discussed his ultimate goals. We already had the land survey, Belle did a land evaluation and had created a property valuation we thought Odell would agree to.

He did. "I think this should work out just fine. What, with Sonny out of the picture, I don't think I need to worry none about his property complaints hurting my sale."

"Funny you should mention that. I did an extensive search, and the Georgia Historical Society discovered property maps that showed the property lines were manipulated in the Pickett's favor. The corrected maps were filed by the attorney for the trust and the property is going back on the market with the new acreage and sales price."

He blinked. "So, what does that mean for Sonny's family?"

"I'm not an attorney, so, I don't really know, but I guess they'll get the land."

He nodded. "Sounds about right to me." A slight laugh gurgled from his throat. "Who'd have thunk it? All these years, and the Pickett's ended up lying the whole time." He scratched his ear. "Kind of makes you wonder what else ain't true? You know what I'm saying?"

I knew exactly what he was saying.

We finished signing the paperwork. With everything on the up and up, I took a handful of photos, but since Odell intended to sell the property to the same builder purchasing Myrtle's property if possible, we didn't focus on the inside of the home.

While outside snapping photos, I caught a glimpse of Junior Goodson in the wooded area of Myrtle's property. Shovel in hand, he dug near the River Birch trees separating Myrtle's property from Sonny Waddell's.

I watched him for a good five minutes and saw no rhyme or reason to his digging. He wasn't doing work. He was searching for the money. I called the attorney and asked if Junior was still scheduled to work on the property. When he answered no, I knew something was up and decided to find out what. Since I had to prep the property for sale again anyway, I had a right to be on the property, and a right to ask what he was doing.

His pickup was parked in the back behind Myrtle's old farm equipment shed, which explained why I didn't see it in the drive when I got to Odell's place. Junior had earbuds in, and I startled him when I tapped on his shoulder.

He pulled a bud from his right ear. "You nearly sent me to the moon, Lilybit." He slammed the shovel tip into the ground and rested his elbow on the handle. "What can I do you for?"

I held the key box up. "Property's going back on the market, so I'm here to put the box back on the door and put the signs up. Saw you out here and wanted to see what's going on. The attorney for the trust said you finished up the other day."

His eyes darted to the house and then back to me. "I'm just finishing up a few things, is all."

I ran my hand down the shovel's long shaft and smiled as I kept my eyes focused on

Junior's the whole time. "Finishing up a few things? Like, one last dig for some buried money maybe?"

He scratched his arm. "You don't really believe that old rumor do you?"

I pointed to the trees. "Weren't you finishing up the work on these the other day?"

His body went rigid, and his expression soured. "I wasn't satisfied with the work, so I came back to do a better job. I take pride in what I do, and if I don't do my best, I got to make it right."

I nodded and peeled a piece of the white and brown bark from one of the trees. "I thought you said these were dying?" I held the bark up and examined it. "Looks pretty alive to me." I glanced at the rest of the four trees. "In fact, they all seem to be pretty alive, and I don't think you've removed any of these." I made a show of checking the area for other River birch trees. "What trees have you removed?"

His face reddened. "There's a bunch of these in the wooded area back there." He pointed to the woods. "You want me to show you?"

I backed up. "Nope. I'm good. Like I said though, I spoke to the attorney handling the trust, and he doesn't want you working on the property for the time being. If you'd like to contact him, we can call him together." I removed my phone from my pocket, where I'd put it when I walked over, and held it out to him. "What do you think?"

He glared at me and then he yanked the shovel from the ground and marched to his truck. I made a show of walking the property, pretending to take photos, hollering out a comment or two about his great job maintaining the land, even though it had been all but destroyed from digging I was almost one hundred percent sure he'd done.

"The grass looks really healthy. Hey, did I mention Odell Luna's property is going on the market now, too?"

He responded with a gruntish sounding mumble.

"Oh, by the way," I walked back to the trees dividing the Waddell land from Myrtle's. "Previous records show this is actually Sonny Waddell's land." I used the heel of my shoe to dig a small line in the ground. "It's not an exact line, but it's right about here somewhere, so you might not want to dig around here for that money anymore, just in case his kids decide they don't want their property messed with."

Junior tapped something into his phone while I headed to the front of the house to hook the key box to the front door.

* * *

I peeked into the front window just because I couldn't stand not knowing how much worse the inside was. I knew if Junior was out digging in back, he'd more than likely been searching inside for the money, too. When I heard someone in the house, I figured it was him and couldn't believe he'd actually have the guts to go in after I told him the attorney no longer needed him.

I entered through the front door and saw Junior down the hall in the kitchen, so, I worked my way through the obstacle course that used to be Myrtle's home and prepared myself to use my firm voice with Junior Goodson, only when I heard another voice, I realized he wasn't alone, and I hid behind Myrtle's old china hutch in the hallway and listened.

"We got to go. I'm telling you, she knows I'm looking for the money. Come on."

"Just a minute," the muffled voice said. "I think I've got—" Something fell and made a loud, vibrating banging sound, which was followed by an even louder feminine scream.

I tucked myself further behind the cabinet. I recognized that voice, but I couldn't quite put my finger on it.

"Dang it, I worked hard to grow these nails," the voice said.

I peeked around the corner and saw Grace Jeffers using a stainless-steel nail file on a nail.

I stepped into the room, my cell phone securely in my hand, tucked into my pocket. "Okay guys, as the realtor for the property, I'm going to have to ask you to leave. I'm calling a locksmith to change the locks, and I'll have the windows secured because this is ridiculous. We don't even know if there's any money hidden here, and you know what, if there is, it's not yours to keep anyway."

Grace's face went from pink to red then to darker than a roasted tomato. She leaned against Myrtle's kitchen counter. "If there's money here, then it belongs to me, and I'm going to find it. I don't care what you have to say about it." Junior grabbed her arm and squeezed, but she yanked it away. "Stop it, Junior."

My head flinched back just a bit. "What are you talking about Grace?"

"You know what I'm talking about. I warned you, and you didn't listen."

"What do you mean, you warned me?"

"I told you to make sure that property didn't sell, but here you are, putting those signs up all over again."

She stepped forward, and that's when I noticed the cast iron skillet in her hand. I pulled my phone out of my pocket, quickly glanced at it and calmly used my thumb to hit the number Belle had assigned Dylan in my favorites. I silently thanked her for that and praised myself for putting my phone on silent. I held both of my hands up in the air, the phone facing behind me. "Come on Grace, you don't want to do this. This isn't your house. It's Myrtle's. Put the skillet down." I glanced at the clock on Myrtle's floor, the one that had been on her wall. If it was still working properly, and if Dylan was at the Sheriff's Office, he'd get to Myrtle's in less than ten minutes, so all I had to do was keep Grace talking and I'd be okay.

I hoped.

How could I have missed what was right in front of me? It all came together when I saw the dried mud hanging from the bottom of her Timberland boot. The mud. The note. The rumor about Jesse's father having a daughter. "You think it's you, don't you?" I turned to Junior. "Or do you? Did you convince her it's her?"

He laughed, the confidence in his laughter bellowing directly at me.

"I know it's me." She lifted her chin. "Look at my face. I look just like a Pickett. Can't you see it? I got the same nose and the same eyes. No matter what my momma says, it's me."

I didn't see any resemblance, but I wasn't about to say that. "How did you get inside my house?"

Her eyes shifted to the nail file on the counter. "You can Google anything these days."

I flicked my head toward Junior. "He told you, didn't he?"

Junior glared at me again.

"That's why you and Jesse kept fighting. You told him you thought it was Grace, too. And he refused to believe you. You wanted the money, so you told her, and you killed Myrtle to get it, didn't you?"

Junior stiffened.

"He didn't kill that old woman, I did, and I made sure it looked like everyone else could have done it, too. I'm not some dumb country girl that's going nowhere. I'm not my momma. I'm taking what's rightfully mine and I'm leaving this dump."

Dylan walked in, his gun drawn and aimed right at Grace Jeffers. "I don't think that's how this works."

I dropped my arms and fell against what was left of the back wall. "Thank God."

Junior threw his arms up in the air, but Grace charged Dylan, the skillet raised high above her head. Dylan aimed the gun at it and fired. The bullet hit the skillet, ricocheted off and zigzagged across the room, hitting a few somethings, though I wasn't sure what, while everyone fell behind what they could to cover themselves. Dylan threw himself in front of me. All the while, the sound of the bullet hitting things in Myrtle Redbecker's kitchen echoed through the room until it stopped, and Grace Jeffers screamed. "I've been shot!"

* * *

Dylan pushed himself up and brushed the hair from my face. "You okay?"

I rubbed my right ankle. "I'm fine, but I think I sprained my ankle."

"Stay here."

He called on the mic on his shirt, and the next hour went by in a few minutes. Billy Ray gave me a big glass of sweet tea, which I happily guzzled down and asked for another. He put two Band-Aids on my ankle, and even though they did nothing physically, I did feel a bit more perky emotionally, so I guess there was something to his method after all.

Dylan cuffed and arrested both Junior and Grace Jeffers. Junior promptly threw his girlfriend under the bus, confessing to being an accessory to both Myrtle and Jesse's murders, but detailing out how Grace planned and carried both out, even going as far as to explain how she lied and said she didn't see Sonny Waddell when she did, and that she saw Odell leave the shovel, when she was the one that had left it because she'd used it to dig around the River birches after she killed Myrtle.

Grace screamed and cried, claiming the money was rightfully hers since she was a Pickett by blood, but Dylan assured her there was an easy way to determine that, and it was called DNA testing. I just wasn't sure it was something that would ever be done.

He insisted I get checked out at the hospital, so I did, even though I didn't think it was necessary. They x-rayed my foot, found nothing but a sprained ankle like I'd said, but the emergency room doctor decided to keep me over night because my blood pressure refused to drop to a reasonably low level and he wanted to keep me for observation. I called Belle to schedule a pick up for the morning. "The doctor says I can't drive for a few days, and he's keeping me overnight. Can you get me tomorrow morning?"

"Why is he keeping you? Are you okay?"

"I'm fine, but my blood pressure isn't cooperating, so he wants to keep me overnight just in case."

"That's worrisome, but okay. But I don't need to get you. Someone is already in the waiting room."

"Who?" A smile filled my face. I tried to make it go away, but my mouth had other plans.

"I think you know the answer to that."

"How do you know?"

"He called me and told me he would hang out there and give you a ride home. You might want to let him know you're going to be staying the night though."

"When did he get here?"

"Same time you did. He followed the ambulance."

The smile grew. "Seriously?"

"When are you going to realize the guy is still in love with you?"

Maybe right then, but I didn't say that.

"I'll see you at your place tomorrow. I want you to meet someone."

"Oh yay, I get to meet Matt. Oh wait. I'm going to ask Dylan to run me to my car and the bank. I need to take care of Myrtle's boxes. I've waited long enough."

"Got it. Text me when you're heading there, and I'll swing by."

We hung up, and I was excited, though I couldn't decide if that was because Dylan was in the waiting room, or because I would soon meet Matt, someone I had a feeling would be around for a long time. I hit the call button and asked if I could see the cute sheriff in the waiting room.

* * *

The doctor released me early the next morning when my blood pressure had been steady at 107 over 71. Dylan had stayed until well past visiting hours, and he promised to pick up Myrtle's boxes from my car before coming back to take me to the bank and then home.

We drove home with my foot wrapped in a big bandage and supported by a pillow in the backseat of his sheriff's car. I felt both excited and embarrassed to be in it, but mostly excited. How often does a girl get to ride in a cop car but not be under arrest? He even put on the lights for me when I asked, though not for long because it went against county laws.

It didn't go unnoticed that the sheriff broke the law for me.

I wobbled into the bank on a set of crutches I already hated and handed the bank manager the information from Myrtle.

"I don't need anything," he said. "She'd already made arrangements."

He removed a letter from a locked drawer in his desk. "I've been expecting you all week." He handed me the letter. "There's a key inside the envelope. It should open the smaller of the lock boxes. The key to the second one is in the first."

Myrtle had taken care to make sure everything was handled properly. I gave her points for her organization skills.

I opened the letter, followed the simple instructions and opened the box. In it was just the key to the second box and a small handwritten note. *If the second box ever goes missing,* the note read, *then whoever opens this is out of luck, and the joke's on everyone.*

"What does that mean?" I asked Dylan.

"It means open the second box."

So, I did. Inside of it was another letter in an old yellowed envelope. I opened it and read it to myself. I stared at Dylan. "God Bless. You're not going to believe it." I handed him the note.

"Boone Pickett had a sense of humor, didn't he?"

We made one more stop at my request before heading to my house.

* * *

Belle sat on my front porch waiting for us when we arrived, but Matt wasn't with her. I wobbled on crutches in her direction. "Don't come all the way here. Just go to the kitchen door," she said.

I ambled that direction, relieved I didn't have to go so far. Crutches weren't fun, and I wasn't going to enjoy the next few days, but Myrtle and Jesse could rest in peace knowing their murderer was behind bars, and Sonny Waddell would be set free, his land rightfully his, and life would be back to normal soon, so I really couldn't complain.

The neighbor's dog barked, only the barked sounded more like a yelp. Belle smiled and clapped. "Oh my gosh, I can't stand it anymore. Matt, bring him."

A tall, dark haired man appeared from my back yard carrying the sweetest puppy in the world. A jiggling, wormy beige little Boxer mix named Sparky wiggled from his grip, fell to the ground and rushed over to me. I nearly fell down next to him. "What? How did you—I thought he'd been adopted?"

"Happy birthday!" Belle screamed. "And he was, but would you believe they returned him the day after you went there? Apparently, their little boy sneezed up a storm so they figured he was allergic to him, and they had to bring him back. They called me because I'd already been there about him before you were and I'd left my number—unlike you—so I went and got him." She rubbed Sparky's heart shaped nose. "He stayed with Matt the night I went to the city."

"He's a good little guy," Matt said. "You got a name for him?"

Dylan had grabbed a chair from my back yard and I sat. He put the wiggly mess of love on my lap, and that mess put his front paws on my chest and showered my face in kisses. "You are so much better than a fish little guy."

He gave me a full-blown French kiss. I didn't complain one bit.

Belle coughed. "Ew. That might be a bit much on the first date."

We laughed.

"Bo can get away with it." I rubbed his ears. "Bo, yes. That's your name little guy. You just look like a Bo."

Belle kissed the top of his head. "I love that."

Matt whispered in her ear.

"Oh, yes please. Thank you."

"We've got a bunch of stuff for you in the car. We'll get it out and put together for you since you're one-legging it right now. In fact," she starred at Dylan. "You might want to stick around for the night to help her take him out." She winked at him.

I coughed. "Smooth move there, bestie."

I filled Belle in on the lock boxes.

"So you're saying there never was any money? That Boone Pickett made the whole thing up?"

"Based on the letter in the box, it would appear so."

"You really think he wrote the letter?"

I nodded, and I showed her a file of letters from Myrtle's house. "We picked these up on the way here. They were in the attic and are items that belonged to Boone. I'm not one hundred percent sure, but I can check other records, and I'm pretty sure I'll find that it's his handwriting. He must have thought the town would get a kick out of the joke."

"Or he was just a mean-spirited old man."

"Or that," I agreed.

Bo showered my face with kisses again.

"Are you going to let the town know?"

"I'm emailing the county paper in a bit. With an image of the letter just in case."

"Good idea."

An hour later both Bo and I were sound asleep on the couch, my leg resting on Dylan's lap, and Bo draped over my chest. My little bungalow never felt more like home. Bo snored in my ear and jolted me out of my slumber.

Dylan laughed. "That's probably the sweetest picture I've seen since you drooled in your sleep in my dorm room my sophomore year at UGA."

I wiped my mouth just in case. "I can't believe you remember that."

Bo stretched and fell off my chest onto the floor. It didn't faze the little guy. He went on a sniffing mission across the room. I kept my eye on him just in case he needed to potty.

"I remember everything, Little Bean." He moved my legs to the table in front of the couch so I could sit up. "And I'm hoping we can make more memories."

He'd worn me down, and no matter how much I wanted to fight my feelings, I didn't have the strength. Who was I kidding? I didn't want to fight my feelings anymore. I wanted to melt into them, to drown in them. "I'd like that, too."

He moved closer. "Really?"

I moved closer, too. "Really." I leaned my head on his shoulder. "But I need to take it slow."

He angled toward me, lifting my head in the process. "I can do that." He tipped my chin forward and gently pressed his lips into mine.

I closed my eyes and let the kiss happen. It was quick and light, and fireworks exploded around us, though I wasn't sure anyone felt or heard them but me.

"Wow. Some things never change," he said.

"What do you mean?"

"Your lips feel just like I remembered."

I smiled. "So do yours." I moved over and leaned my head back on his shoulder. "It's kind of sad though."

"What is?"

"Bo is a much better kisser than you."

THE END

Keep Reading for chapter one of Decluttered and Dead book two in the Lily Sprayberry Realtor Cozy Mystery Series Available September 2018

DECLUTTERED AND DEAD

A LILY SPRAYBERRY REALTOR COZY MYSTERY

CHAPTER ONE

"Bo, heel." I stood ramrod straight with the vibration controller in hand, ready to press the button on my Boxer mix puppy's collar if he didn't heel to my side. His crazy-legged gallop, the one where his big feet flopped all over the place from pure uncontrollable excitement, screeched to a halt, and he backed up, placing himself into the heeled position by my right side.

I beamed with pride. Bo was only four months old, but he'd already grown out of his puppy stage and into a clumsy forty-pound lump of drooling, rock-like muscle lap dog. The muscle that left a multi-colored bruise when it plowed into the side of my leg. I'd started the two of us in training, and so far, we'd done well. Actually, Bo did better than me. I was a softy, and I needed to toughen up so he didn't get mixed signals. It wasn't easy though, with those big puppy eyes staring at me as they did.

We stayed in heel position until we walked closer to the dog park entrance inside Castleberry Park. Bo's tail wagged blissfully, and he stuck his little booty in the air with his front paws down, in what I called his puppy play mode, when he saw all of his friends rush to the fence to bark their hellos. "Bo, sit."

He sat.

I completely understood how parents felt when their kids did something wonderful. Sure, Bo wasn't a human kid, but he was my baby, and for me, the fact that he had four legs and a tail didn't matter. His daily accomplishments were also mine, and they made me happy. I removed the leash and said okay, and he rushed off to the fence gate.

Another dog owner opened it, greeted Bo with a cheerful hello and pat on the head, which he acknowledged with a tag wag and then bolted off to play.

After thirty minutes of tumbling and rough-housing with the other dogs, I had to drag him out practically kicking and screaming like a toddler. We needed to practice our off-leash training on the park's path before meeting the not-yet-labeled man in my life, Dylan Roberts.

Castleberry Park was the largest of three Bramblett County recreational parks. The county built it two years ago to accommodate the increased popularity of lacrosse and teams from all over the state flocked to tournaments there every season except winter because it was the only one in northern Georgia with eleven turf lacrosse fields. With the pressure of local dog owners, the county added the dog park to an unused, lightly wooded area about nine months ago. The paved multi-use path outlining the park was perfect for practicing off leash training with Bo. Though technically the law stated all dogs must be on a leash no longer than six feet, it was early enough that the morning walkers didn't complain, and since the not-yet-defined man in my life just happened to be the county Sheriff, I flat out broke that law. I figured I'd get off with a warning at least the first time I got caught.

In my defense, I wasn't the only one that did it, though my momma would tell me that's no excuse and question if I'd jump off a bridge because everyone did it, but technically speaking, the electronic collar was a leash, and I had more control over Bo with the controller than I did with an actual physical strap, so I would argue that point in court any day if I had to. I just hoped it never came to that.

We'd spent twenty minutes walking part of the two-mile path and made it to the section connecting to the exit path that connected to Gibson Bridge. Nose to the ground, Bo followed a scent to the right and onto that path. The bridge was about a half mile up and it was his most favorite place on earth. An ideal spot for local photographers and artists, the old covered wood walking bridge didn't actually lead anywhere anymore unless one wanted to cross the rocky stream to fish or swim. Bo liked to watch the fish jump out of the water. They fascinated him. He'd try to catch them with his drooling mouth and droopy jowls, but wasn't quick enough.

The covered section of the bridge was my favorite place to hang out, mostly because of the shade. It leaned just a bit to the left, and years of teenagers carving their true loves names into the old wood was considered damage by some, but I thought of it as a touch of history and nostalgia. Yes, Dylan and I had our names carved into it, too, which was why I thought of the carvings as nostalgic rather than damaging. Our long-term high school and college relationship had been intense and hadn't ended well, but he wanted to give it another try, and considering I was still in love with him, I couldn't deny the chance. I just had to take it slow because I didn't trust that he wouldn't up and leave me again.

"You feel like going that way, big guy?" I checked my watch. We still had a good fifteen minutes before we had to meet Dylan, so I figured why not?

I sent Dylan a quick text telling him we'd veered off toward the bridge and might be a few minutes late just in case.

"The nose goes where the nose goes," he replied.

Up ahead I caught a glimpse of my high school friend and college sorority sister, Heather Barrington walking with a man with short brown hair and a scruffy beard I thought looked like William Abernathy. William's family owned the biggest and most popular corn maze and pumpkin patch in the surrounding area. Another high school and college friend, Caroline Abernathy, married William shortly after college. As I walked Bo toward them, the man turned off the path and cut through the wooded section.

Heather and Caroline were best friends then, and best friends still, and both were signed up to be in my Decluttering and Staging Your Home for Sale class starting later that morning.

Bo greeted Heather with a nose bump to a somewhat private place. He had no shame, but it embarrassed me. "Bo, heel."

He backed up and stood by my side.

"Sorry about that. We're still learning our manners."

She waved it off. "Oh, honey, he's a dog. That's how they say hey." She bent down and patted Bo's head. "I'm looking forward to class today. Should be a lot of fun. Will Belle be there?"

Belle Pyott, my best friend and business partner, also went to school with Heather and me.

"She'll come by, but she's not staying for the entire class."

She blew out a breath and puffed her bottom lip out into a pout. "That's too bad. Funny, we all live in the same town and rarely see each other."

"Caroline will be there, too, but you probably already knew that. Hey, was that William I just saw with you?"

She twirled a strand of her long red hair around her finger. "William? Oh, heavens, no. That was a client. He's looking for a painting of the bridge. Wanted to see if I was interested in doing one for him."

I nodded even though it sure looked like William to me.

We caught up as we walked toward the main path. "Well, I have to meet someone, but I'll see you an hour or so," I said.

She smiled. "Yes, I hear you're back together with Dylan. You sure latched onto that tall drink of water right quick when he got back to town."

And that's when I remembered why we'd stopped hanging out. My momma once said there were two types of women, One type, a man brings home to his momma, and the other type a man brings home, but not to the house his momma lived in. She also said girls went to college for one of two types of degrees, either a degree from the university itself or an M-R-S degree. She believed Heather Barrington went to college thinking she was the bring her home to momma kind of girl and wanted that M-R-S degree, but when she realized that wasn't in the cards, she'd flipped sides. Based on Heather's comment, I had to agree with my momma.

I didn't want her to make a play for Dylan, not that I thought he'd fall for it, but because we'd been friends since elementary school. That would be all kinds of awkward, her throwing herself into the mix of my sort of relationship with my one true love, but I also didn't feel right saying something that wasn't entirely true. "We're testing the waters." The truth was, yes, Dylan was back in town, and yes, we were spending time together, but the relationship itself hadn't yet been defined. I knew I loved him. I'd always loved him, but slow and steady won the race, and I was in no hurry to get to the finish line. Thankfully, Dylan understood.

"Well, that boy's got a mighty fine physique to go swimming with. He's all grown up now, that's for sure." She giggled, but it was more of an evil laugh than one filled with humor. "Keep an eye on that one. Someone might just sneak up behind you and steal him out from under you if you don't."

Gee, was that a threat of some sort? Had she let me know she'd planned to make a play for my man? Was he even really my man? Ugh. As if I needed that kind of additional stress in my life, especially given the fact that Heather would be in my face every day for the next week.

"Ta ta," she said, heading in the other direction. She turned around a second or two later. "Oh, Lily, I'd be tickled pink if you'd put one of my paintings up in your office. I'm into reds right now. They really add a pop of color." She wiggled her head and flicked her hair back. "I mean, look at my hair. Men just adore it, and you know what they say about us gingers. I bet one of my paintings would bring in all kinds of business."

Did she actually just threaten to take my man and then try to sell me her artwork? Wow. If I remembered correctly, the saying about gingers referred to them having no souls, though I doubted that's the one she meant.

Bless her heart. She wanted to sell her work so bad she'd resorted to comparing it to her floosy ways. I had half a mind to tell her that sales technique wouldn't work on women, but she might could give it a try on some of the older men in town. I would have bet good money on Old Man Goodson buying her self-portrait and hanging it right next to the 50s girl pin up calendar in his shop.

If my momma knew what I was thinking she'd have sent me outside to pick the thinnest switch on a tree in my backyard and then whacked me on the back of the thighs with it. I was ashamed of myself for my nasty thoughts, especially because they were about an old friend.

I didn't want one of Heather's paintings, but I almost pitied her because I knew her life hadn't turned out the way she'd expected. Heather planned to marry rich and paint without worry of supporting herself. Instead, she still lived at home with her parents and worked at their store while trying to sell her paintings on the side. That had to crush the ego. "I'll talk to Belle, see what we can do." I smiled, knowing Belle thought a blind cow could paint better than our old friend. Belle didn't have an eye for art. It wasn't just Heather's. "See you in a bit."

She waved and skipped off. "Ta ta, love."

Bo and I met up with Dylan a few minutes later.

"Why the long face?" he asked.

I ignored the old joke reference that referred to the person resembling a horse because I knew he hadn't gone there. "I just ran into Heather Barrington."

"And?"

"I suggest you watch your back."

He glanced behind him. "Hard to do when it's behind me."

I rolled my eyes. "You know what I mean."

"Okay. Done. Care to tell me why though?"

"Because she'll probably leave claw marks in it if you don't."

"Noted." He brushed the back of his hand across my face. "Did you tell her I only have eyes for you?"

"I didn't think that would be appropriate."

"Then I promise, if she tries to get her claws into me, I'll make sure she knows."

I had a feeling the sheriff's office wouldn't have any Heather Barrington original artwork hanging in it any time soon.

"So, you know that secret client I've been working with for the past two weeks?"

He nodded. "The one that's taken you away from your favorite crime TV shows?"

"I have cable, you know. I can watch them on On Demand."

"That's too bad. You also have a real-life crime fighter right here." He pointed to his chest, which, I had to admit, was quite sexy in the tight-fitting t-shirt stuck to him from the sweat of his run.

"You're a small-town sheriff. The crime rate here is what, negative twenty?"

"It went up with the two murders you were involved in, remember?"

"I wasn't actually involved in them."

The corner of his mouth twitched, and I nearly melted right there. "So, go on."

"Okay, so this client is an old friend." I tapped the side of my leg, and Bo heeled to me. I wanted to do my happy dance, but per the trainer, I acted like it was no big deal. "And she's back in town to help sell her parent's house, so she's decided to go ahead and take my decluttering class even though we've finished the job on her parents place already."

"That's odd. Did you not do a good job on the place?"

I nudged him with my shoulder. "Of course I did. That's not why she's taking it. She was scheduled in it anyway, but I think she's taking it because of the other people registered. I'm pretty sure he wants to make a statement."

"Who is it?"

"Someone that's going to make my life miserable and cause some a ton of conflict in the class just by showing up."

I could almost see his brain working. Dylan also grew up in Bramblett County, and he knew everyone I knew, so it took him less than a minute to figure it out.

He laughed. "You've got to be kidding me? Savannah Emmerson?"

I nodded. "Belle set this up. I think she does this stuff to me on purpose."

"Belle Of course she does." He laughed harder. "That's hilarious. It's going to be a train wreck. I can't believe you're going through with it."

"What other option do I have?"

"You could tell her not to come."

"That wouldn't be very nice. Besides, she's offered to use her parent's house as an example for the class, and it looks great. Belle and I are even using it in our company portfolio. What am I supposed to do, say thanks for letting us use your folks home for our stuff, but hey, you're not welcome to the class because you're a floosy and pretty much everyone in the class hates you?"

"Maybe if you chose better words?"

I bowed my head and moaned. "This is going to be a disaster."

Savannah, Caroline, Heather, Belle, and I all hung out in the same social circle growing up, and in college, the five of us joined the same sorority at the University of Georgia. Things were great for a short time there, but Savannah ripped the group to shreds when she slept with Heather's boyfriend, Austin Emmerson, our sophomore year at UGA. Rumor had it she also slept with Caroline's boyfriend, now husband, but that was never confirmed. Savannah eventually married Austin and moved to Atlanta. In the process of a divorce, she came back to Bramblett County under the guise of helping her parents get their house organized and sold while they headed north to their retirement home in Maine. That's when she hired me and when Belle decided to sign her up for the decluttering class.

"Do you want me to send a deputy to make sure no fights break out?" The mouth twitch thing happened again.

"Don't joke. I might seriously need that."

We walked with Bo between us. "Makes sense now."

"What?"

"I ran into Austin Emmerson last night at Willy's."

"Really? Did he say anything?"

"About what?"

"The divorce."

"Sort of. He said something about a fight they'd had, how she'd screwed him out of a lot of money, but that's about it. I figured he was just blowing off steam."

"She hasn't really said much to me. You know how rumors spread around here, she probably wants to keep it on the downlow."

"Especially about her."

We made it back to the parking lot where he'd parked his black, four-door sheriff's car next to my car. "My poor car."

"What? Your car is great," he said.

"Next to your monstrosity it looks like one of those little Matchbox cars." I rubbed the roof. "I feel bad for it."

"I'm the sheriff. I need a big, manly car. Image is everything."

I laughed. "If that's true, then I'm a dainty little southern gal."

He kissed my forehead. "And that's what I love best about you."

I blushed. His expression was sincere, while I'd been kidding. I'd not really thought of myself as dainty, so it surprised me to think he did. "Thank you for taking Bo to doggy daycare today. I appreciate it." I hugged and kissed my puppy goodbye.

"Anything to win points with the mutt." He kissed my forehead again as Bo jumped into the back of his vehicle. "And you, of course."

I hadn't told him yet, but he'd already won back most of the points he'd lost years ago. "Okay, I'm off to get ready to referee this class. Stopping at the office and then getting some treats at Millie's first. Hopefully, that'll ease the shock when Savannah walks in."

"Good luck."

"Thanks, I'm going to need it." I blew him a kiss as he pulled away.

* * *

I'd pre-ordered a variety of baked goods and two jugs of sweet tea from Millie's, so they'd be ready for pick up when I stopped by. The county library where we'd decided to hold the decluttering class was a just hop away from the bakery café, which was just another hop away from my office, but since I had all of the materials for the class along with the food and drinks, I still needed to drive. I loaded the yummy baked goods into my car and headed the block to the library.

The library was in desperate need of an update. I loved the smell and feel of old libraries. Their walls filled from floor to ceiling with shelves of books. I could wander the sectioned areas, run my fingertips across the spines of old hardcovers and paperbacks, breathe in the smell of the ink and paper.

The Bramblett County library lacked the character of an old library, the kind writers flocked to for research and readers went to just to soak in the environment, to be one with the written word. It just mechanical, necessary even, and felt old and dingy. The incandescent lighting gave the white walls a yellowish hue, though I suspected they were that way also because they needed a fresh coat of paint. The bookshelves weren't the dark, antique kind one might find in a big city library, but rather the kind from a retro 70s library, created by some art deco designer with an addiction to maple wood. And the place didn't smell like old books. It smelled like burnt coffee. Every time I walked in, I was immediately disappointed. I knew what awaited me inside, but nonetheless, I expected something different, and every time, I ended up disappointed.

The head librarian, Ellie Jean Pruitt, who'd also been my high school librarian, greeted me at the front desk. "Well, hey there, Miss Lilybit. I got the conference room all set up for you." She walked from behind the library front desk and picked up one of my bags. "Let me help you with that. Follow me, and I'll show you where you're going to be for the next few days."

"Thank you so much."

Ellie Jean had a daughter named Faith. She was my age, so Ellie Jean had to have been around my parent's age, but you wouldn't know it by looking at her. She fit the typical librarian stereotype. Old lady glasses with little points on the sides, her graying hair pulled into a tight bun and a floral print dress that fit her like a potato sack. It hit her larger than normal chest and hung down, without any shape, to her knees. She'd been married once, but her husband left town when their daughter was two and never returned. I couldn't help but think it was because of the potato sack dresses, but I kept that thought to myself.

Like my momma always said, if you can't say something nice, shut your pie hole.

Granted, she said that in the privacy of our home, and mostly to my brothers, but her words stuck with me, too.

"You're going to be in this room here." She opened the door to a plain but bright room, at least bright in comparison to the rest of the place. The back wall was actually the side of the building and lined with windows, allowing in nice natural light.

I glanced down at the chairs. The red cushions had faded from the sun. "If you keep the blinds closed when no one's using the room, the color on the cushions won't fade as quickly."

"Oh dear." She pulled out a chair and gasped. "They really are faded, aren't they? I'll have to talk to the board about replacing them."

Belle showed up a few minutes after I finished setting up the conference room. That wasn't unusual for her. I wasn't always prompt—one of my annoying bad habits—but Belle rarely arrived on time. I made a point of telling her events began thirty minutes early when I needed her there on time. The decluttering class set-up though, I could handle on my own. Besides, she organized the class, so I couldn't fudge the start time without her catching on.

She plopped into a chair and fanned herself, her long black hair pulled into a clip instead of styled to the hilt as usual. I eyed her up and down, and she caught on quickly. "Do not start with me. I barely slept a wink last night."

"If you're going to hoot with the owls, you'd better be able to soar with the eagles the next day."

"Honey, this gal did no hooting last night. I had a sinus headache the size of Killamon-whatever it's called. What in heaven's name is up with this weather anyway? My poor nose can't figure out if it should be clear or clogged."

"It's horrible, I'll give you that."

She rubbed her temples. "Stop talking so loud." She glanced at me with her blood shot eyes. "Do you have sinus medicine or anything I can take? My head is pounding?"

I laughed. "You sure are a hot mess." I pointed to the other side of the room where I'd set my bag. "I think I've got something in there."

She dragged herself to my bag. "Hey, I forgot to tell you who I saw over at the old First Baptist Church yesterday."

"Who?"

"William Abernathy."

"Really? That's odd."

"What's even more odd is he was walking out of it with Heather Barrington."

"That's interesting."

"Yeah, why?" She tossed the pills into her mouth and swallowed them down with a swig of her coffee.

"Because I saw him this morning with Heather, too. Except he took off when I got close, and when I asked Heather if it was him, she said it wasn't."

"Hmm. Wonder what that means?"

"It means this class is going to be interesting, that's for sure."

"Well, we already knew that, considering who's going to be in it."

"Yes, I just hope they don't wind up killing each other."

* * *

The girl's arrived one by one, ready to hit the ground running. Caroline, then Heather, and the two older women who'd signed up for the class, Bonnie Bass, and Henrietta Harvey.

Finally, after we'd all settled in and class started, Savannah made her grand entrance.

And grand it was, plus totally intentional.

"I'm sorry I'm late," she said, bursting into the conference room as if everyone knew she'd be there.

Both Heather and Caroline gasped. Belle snickered, her headache apparently better.

"You better not leave now," I whispered to Belle.

A big grin stretched across her face. "And miss this little catawampus? No way, baby."

"You have the face of an angel and the soul of a sinner."

"My momma says that, too."

"Where do you think I got it?"

Heather pushed her chair back from the conference room table. "Lily Sprayberry, what were you thinking, inviting this…this hussy into here like this?" She shot out of her seat and marched to the door. "If she's here, I…I just can't be a part of this. You know what she did to me."

I whispered out of the corner of my mouth to Belle. "Soul of a sinner for sure." I cut Heather off before she left. "Heather, wait."

"Oh, for heaven's sake, don't pitch a fit because of me," Savannah said. "You think I need a class like this? Sweetie, I live in Buckhead. I have people that declutter and organize for me. I don't need to do it myself."

Except she just spent the last two weeks doing it at her parent's house, so that didn't really make sense, unless it was because her parents were paying for it and not her rich husband or in-laws.

I breathed a sigh of relief knowing she was leaving, but Belle's eyes about popped out of her head in utter disappointment. "What do you mean? You're signed up for the class."

She wiggled her designer purse and flung it over her shoulder. "Why would I waste my time drinking cheap sweat tea with—" She waved her hand across the room. "With women that hate me? If I'm going to do that, I'll just do it in town with my fake friends there. At least there I'll get a good cup of espresso."

Ouch. Millie's tea was by far the best in the south, and she definitely didn't deserve the criticism from Savannah, whose personality had gone well passed snooty to self-righteous in a hot minute.

"We'd love you to stay," Belle said, and I thought she actually meant it.

"Over my dead body, or better yet, hers," Heather said. "I cannot even consider staying if that hussy stays."

Savannah straightened her shoulders. "Why, I have a mind to—"

Heather pushed up her sleeves. "It's about time we do."

I jumped between them and stretched out my arms, locking my elbows just in case. "Come on already. We're adults. Let's act like it."

"I'm with Heather," Caroline said. "If Savannah thinks she can just waltz in here and act like she didn't try to sleep with my husband, well then—"

"He wasn't your husband at the time," Savannah said.

"I should have brought a bag of microwave popcorn," Henrietta said.

Bonnie dug in her purse. "I might have some in here somewhere." She picked out a bag of crackers, two packs of gum, a makeup bag, her wallet, and then finally huffed and said, "Oh, heavens," and dumped the bag's contents onto the table. After pushing the items around and not finding the popcorn bag, she sighed. "Nope, none."

"That's too bad. This cat fight deserves a good bag of microwave popcorn," Henrietta said.

We'd all watched Bonnie, surprised and bemused by her search for a bag of popcorn in her purse, and when she shoved the items on the table back into her bag, it brought us all back to reality.

Caroline stood and pointed her finger at Savannah. "Oh, darling, he's my husband now, and I'm warning you, you lay one gel nail on my man and you won't live to regret it."

Belle coughed.

"Is everything all right?" Ellie Jean Pruitt asked. She'd been moving the empty chairs away from the table to give us all some extra room when Savannah walked in.

"We're fine, Mrs. Pruitt." I turned to Savannah. "Maybe it's best you don't take the class."

"I never really planned on it. I just wanted to see how my two long lost friends would react when they saw me. But, of course, you can still show my parent's home tomorrow. I'll be there to let you in and then I'll leave so they don't pitch another hissy fit." She plucked a treat from the tray on the table, took a bite, made a scrunched up face and then set the treat back on the tray. "Oh, and Heather, you can have your sweet Austin back. I'm divorcing him. You'll love my sloppy seconds." She smiled at me, and as she walked out, said, "See you tomorrow, lovies. Ta-ta."

Heather hollered after her. "He was my sloppy seconds first."

"That went well," Belle said and took a sip of her tea.

"That…that, well, I just can't use the kind of words I want because I'm a lady, but let me tell you, she's about as welcome in this town as an outhouse breeze," Caroline said.

That was probably one of the worst insults one could give a southern woman, and I thanked the Lord above Savannah wasn't there to hear it.

I stood staring at the other clients in the room. Bonnie and Henrietta gave each other a knowing glance. Ellie Jean fussed with the chairs, and Caroline and Heather shot daggers at me. I tapped my pencil on the conference room table, both to get everyone's attention and to focus my thoughts on how to start the class. "So, there are four key elements to decluttering and staging a home." I figured it was best to pretend nothing had happened and just move forward.

"That little hussy makes me so mad I could spit nails," Heather said.

"And to think she just walks in here like she never slept with our men," Caroline added.

"She didn't just sleep with my man, Caroline. She married him."

"Well, at least you found out before you married him. Imagine how that could have turned out," Caroline added.

"I couldn't marry him because he dumped me for her."

"Exactly. Look at me. I'll never know if my William slept with her for sure or not. He won't say, and now I'm married to him without knowing the truth." She fell into her seat and fanned her face with the packet full of papers I'd provided. "And heaven help her, if she even goes near my William, she won't see the light of day."

If the rest of my week went like the first fifteen minutes of class, heaven help me. "Ladies, how about we focus on why we're here instead of digging up the past?"

"Absolutely," Belle agreed. "What's done is done. Let's just move on. What do you say?"

"You would say that," Heather said. "The hussy never slept with your boyfriend."

"That's because she had several. Even Savannah would have had a hard time keeping up." Caroline said.

Bonnie hooted. "Ooh wee, she shoots to kill, don't she?"

Henrietta nodded. "Emm, hmm. Reminds me of myself back in the day."

I wanted to duck because I feared Belle would very likely chuck a scone straight at Caroline's face, and I was right in the line of fire. Only she didn't. It had to be because she hadn't slept the night before and was off her game.

I did my best to stop the fighting and regain control of my environment. I singled out Heather and Caroline, making eye contact with both of them. "Okay, that's enough. I've got a class to teach here, so if you two want to talk about this you're going to have to step out and do it elsewhere. The other women in this class didn't pay to listen to you two pitch fits about stuff that happened years ago."

"Oh, it's okay," Henrietta said. "They canceled my soap operas, so this is the next best thing."

Bonnie giggled. "For me, too. I haven't seen something this exciting in months, and I love me a good drama."

"Someone might could tell that one that just left that you can catch more bees with honey than vinegar. Her momma didn't do right by her, I can tell you that."

"Emm hmm," Bonnie said.

Belle bit her bottom lip to stop herself from laughing.

I had to admit, they were two little spitfires. I held back a giggle also. "Thank you for your ability to roll with things, ladies, I appreciate it, but this isn't the time of place for drama." I directed my next comments to my old friends. "So, take your pick ladies. Leave and trash talk, or stay and learn some valuable tools for your future. What's it going to be?"

They both grunted, crossed their arms over their chests and didn't budge. I assumed that meant they'd decided to stay.

We made it through the first day of class without any additional drama, and frankly, I was surprised. I begged the Lord and every deceased real estate agent in the heavens above to help me get through the next day when we all toured Savannah's parent's home. I wanted to finish the tour without any damages to the property, myself, or my clients.

Unfortunately, that prayer went unanswered.

To purchase Decluttered and Dead A Lily Sprayberry Realtor Cozy Mystery visit your favorite online realtor for the paperback, or Amazon for the Kindle version.

ACKNOWLEDGEMENTS

Thank you to my wonderful editor, Jen, my favorite proofreader, JC Wing, my favorite beta reader, Lynn Shaw, and my friends and family who've supported me as I've traveled along this writing journey.

A big thank you to Teri Fish! She picked Bo for the name of Lily's new Boxer mix puppy!

About the Author

Carolyn Ridder Aspenson currently calls the Atlanta suburbs home, but can't rule out her other two homes, Indianapolis and somewhere in the Chicago suburbs.

She is old enough to share her empty nest with her husband, two dogs and two cats, all of which she strongly obsesses over repeatedly noted on her Facebook and Instagram accounts, and is working on forgiving her kids for growing up and leaving the nest. When she is not writing, editing, playing with her animals or contemplating forgiving her kids, she is sitting at Starbucks listening in on people's conversations and taking notes, because that stuff is great for book ideas.

On a more professional note, she is the bestselling author of the Angela Panther cozy mystery series featuring several full-length novels and novellas as well as a collection of romantic novellas.

OTHER BOOKS BY CAROLYN RIDDER ASPENSON

The Angela Panther Contemporary Mystery Series
Unfinished Business
Unbreakable Bonds
Uncharted Territory
Unexpected Outcomes
Unbinding Love
The Christmas Elf
The Ghosts
The Event
Undetermined Events
The Inn at Laurel Creek Contemporary Romance Novella Series
Zoe & Daniel's Story
The Inn at Laurel Creek
The Lily Sprayberry Realtor Cozy Mystery Series
Deal Gone Dead
Decluttered and Dead
The Scarecrow Snuff Out
Sleigh Bells & Sleuthing (A Holiday Author Novella Collection featuring Lily Sprayberry)

Independent Novellas
Santa's Gift A Cumming Christmas Novella

Purchase Carolyn's books through the online retail outlet where you purchased this one.

Made in the USA
Columbia, SC
04 August 2019